About the Author

Peter C. Harley is an Author with a Degree in Surveying who works in the Property Development sector. He resides alone in Nottinghamshire, England, has one daughter who is autistic, a passion for the countryside, animals, classic cars and architecture. His work has the common theme of the inter-connections, intersections and inter-relationships of the journey through life and beyond.

Dedication

To Bambi.
Your unintentional influence, often devoid of mere words, has created the greatest, deepest, inexorable impact within my soul. Always. X

Peter C. Harley

UNDER HER UMBRELLA

AUSTIN MACAULEY
PUBLISHERS LTD.

A CIP catalogue record for this title is available from the British Library.

ISBN 9781785546228 (Paperback)
ISBN 9781785546235 (Hardback)
ISBN 9781785546242 (E-Book)

www.austinmacauley.com

First Published (2016)
Austin Macauley Publishers Ltd.
25 Canada Square
Canary Wharf
London
E14 5LQ

Acknowledgments

Thank you to anyone I have ever come across in life, or in my imagination, no matter what situation that was in. You may have influenced a character, situation or direction. A special thank you to Jean Hall when over from Australia for her encouragement and proof reading of the first draft while I was still writing it.

Chapter 1

Who Lives There?

"Wow! So, who lives in a place like this?" No, not a reference to a popular television series; 'Through the Keyhole'. In the programme, it was the quest of a panel to guess the name of the celebrity whose residence they were being shown footage of. A few clues on which to focus the mind, were strategically placed to assist with the identification of the individual. The privacy of the yet-to-be-identified celebrity was being invaded, not only by the panel, but by millions of the general population sitting before their television screens.

I was beginning to realise how they felt, hearing the question emitted by a lady's voice from the other side of the garden wall. Judging by the voices accompanying her, it was a family on a Sunday afternoon stroll by the river. It is a question however, that is posed by many of the naturally inquisitive population when travelling around the country. The query is usually raised whilst trying to extend their necks in a giraffe-like profile, the purpose of which, being to gain inside knowledge of who resides 'over the wall'. The quest is amplified by any half-reasonable dwelling that they proceed past; the more expensive the dwelling; the more intriguing the question becomes. Of course, while they are undertaking this task, they are simply carrying out their daily business. Well, not so much their business, as trying to interfere, or gain an insight in someone else's business.

Sundays are the worst, when the afternoon boredom takes hold of evolution, merging the human population with the meerkats' animal instinct, all under the pseudo of an interest. The stroll to the pub; countryside walk; cycle ride; or drive, are all no more than an act of fiction undertaken to camouflage the true intent of the journey. We all complain that our lives are too busy, that our minds are always pre-occupied, but what happens when we do gain free time? Simple; we saturate our over-active, inquisitive minds with matters that do not concern us, or impact upon us. We then fill all of the voids within our minds with meaningless information, pouring grains of sand into a jar packed with stones, only to further add a jar of water to ensure complete and total saturation is achieved.

The family had clearly come to rest behind my house. The voices were not moving. I could recognise the sound of a child repeatedly jumping up and down, probably attempting to look over the wall in an attempt to ascertain what our property looks like; their low vantage point obscuring their view. I predicted what was to follow, their father lifting them onto his shoulders to secure an elevated vantage point. Maybe I should install a viewing window within the wall to facilitate their learning.

Well in answer to the question they posed; in the case of this six-bedroom Victorian Gothic House, set in the rural Nottinghamshire countryside, on the bank of the River Trent, it is I. Not that they will manage to further their knowledge to any significance. The original high brick wall concealing two acre surroundings make the viewing problematic, further fuelling the desire to gain said knowledge. The less people can easily discover, the more intriguing the instinct becomes, leading to self-questioning and more than a little fabrication as to the nature of the unfortunate occupant.

"I wonder if it's someone famous?"

The excited sound of a little girl's voice responded, she clearly had no control of her wild imagination. Her voice drilled into me, I was finding the very sound combined with her freedom of speech, rather painful. It was a freedom that almost everyone takes for granted without ever questioning. Responding to the sound of her mother almost instantaneously, reacting to a question, or thought, that had been expressed.

What more plausible explanation could there be? Of course, almost every sizeable property that has a degree of privacy, is occupied by a person earning money from doing what we all do each and every day – pretending to be someone else. Most of us conceal our true being behind an image of false contentment, or appear to be pleasant despite what we may truly be thinking. This is all the mirage that is simply regarded as human nature. If a person does not know something they speculate, fabricate, often leading to assumptions, categorising any individual as a stereotype.

My ornate, black wrought iron gates have metal panels clad behind, and are operated by the obligatory remote controlled motor, adding oxygen to the burning desire of what is simple, human, nosiness. How many people have attempted to hazard a guess at the question that was posed while partaking in the Sunday afternoon activity? This, I will never know. How many have been remotely near to the truth? Well, maybe none. It is not as glamorous as it appears. The rose-coloured spectacles do not apply here, the harsh reality, still casts its ugly shadow through the mirage of affluent bliss.

The property from the front elevation, is something that to be fair, encourages the question from those passing by, teasing the inquisitive mind. The ornate, Victorian dressings; the mullions; transoms; chimneys; pinnacles; arches; balconies and oriel windows. They are rather dramatic; a touch of George Gilbert Scott in a Kings Cross Station style, rather than the mock Glass Reinforced Plastic features of today's imitation features, bolted to the monotonous box. It is built from red brick with stone detailing; its presence stands proud amongst the trees of the landscaped garden.

"I wonder if they have a Ferrari?"

The voice of a little boy piped up, an inquisitor in training. I felt for a moment like shouting back, stating how far he was from the truth. No, totally wrong it is the classic, simple, beginners sports car of the 1960's and 70's – the MG Midget.

Well, three Midgets and the original concept of the car; a 1958 Mk1 Austin Healey Sprite, known affectionately to most as the Frogeye. Why them? Why not? They are fun, have personality and ooze character.

"They will not be famous Chloe; that's stupid! It is a thief; they robbed a bank, then blew the getaway car up."

The little boy had an imagination even wilder than his sister, running free, untamed and closely coupled to his voice. The irony of it all, is that despite that I have never stolen anything, he was a great deal closer to the truth. So close that my mind flashed back to incidents of a few years ago, as well as how my life had changed in the last decade or so.

I continued to pace around the garden, deep in thought, my mind taken over by worry and concern. I was striding out, in some desperate attempt to control the helpless frustration that was expanding within. I crossed the lawn, passing a small folly tower which allowed views over the wall on to the banks of the River Trent, as well as revealing any passing audience.

I entered the residence which within displays an abundance of architectural features, remaining in-keeping with the external environment. No minimalist, contemporary styled rooms, looking as if the furniture had been repossessed, or someone was soon to move in, reside here. Instead, Victorian Gothic in all of the best rooms kept under lock and key, with modern, not over stylised items located in the remaining rooms, beneath a scattering of plastic toys like a snowstorm on a winter's day.

The quiet, away from that passing family came to an abrupt halt, with the sudden outburst of a loud scream emitted from the neighbouring room. The sounds were soon accompanied by the unmistakable, hurtful sound of fist hitting flesh. I rushed through to the adjacent room to establish the cause of the disturbance and calmly, but as firmly as necessary, restrained the perpetrator. The screams then merged with the sound of the battle; a twisting, wriggling, struggle which soon came to an end. I was not overly surprised at this sudden incident; all had remained peaceful and quiet within the house for a good two hours now. Feeling the firm grasp of the clothes on my back, I turned around to face the door into the kitchen. The grasp rapidly changed tactics; clutching my hand, I was pulled towards the corner of the room, accompanied by an infectious, mischievous, chuckle.

My assailant pointed to the CD player in the corner of the room, not to command that I help them remove it from the house, but demanding with an indestructible intensity of focused strong will, that I turned the music on. I freed my hand from the small, vice-like grip and did as I was commanded to keep the peace. The phone rang, but I allowed the call to glide into the answering machine message, I had no option if I was to retain the mood now that the residence had returned to its former tranquillity. The ringing abruptly reconvened, this time the melodious tune of the mobile, displaying the caller's name. A call that I was desperate, bursting to return sooner rather than later. I was all too aware that there was my partner and livelihood at stake.

Was this to be the news that I had been waiting for? I returned the call, on this; a warm, peaceful, calm evening, with a relaxing stillness in the air. An atmosphere that I could detect, despite being the opposite of how I was feeling within. The last glimmer of orange-tinted sunlight was creating silhouettes on the skyline of trees and of the house itself. A Barn Owl made its presence known, swooping across the fields to spot its innocent pray, which had mistakenly ventured out in the last glimmer of light. The darting, swirling movements of a bat flashed past near an outside light, feeding on attracted flies. I sat at the bottom of the tower with a large crystal glass of Laphroaig in hand. The peat smoke aroma of this Islay Malt Whisky, adding an additional dynamic to the senses abundant on this summer evening. I needed the drink, I was unsure what I was about to hear. Mark Daniels familiar, distinctive voice answered the call in a slightly abrupt manner. My anticipation grew, my pounding heart was racing, wondering if there was any news. Mark's voice was becoming warmer when the caller was identified, although remaining to the point.

"How about a classic car trip for you, pal? I'll meet you tomorrow at mine, about eleven."

"Mark, are you serious? I have no time or inclination for this at the moment! For fuck's sake man, is there any news? What can I do to help? Someone must know something with all of your contacts? Surely you can do something? I will do anything, Mark. Absolutely anything."

My outburst of questions erupted, unrestrained from the depths of my soul. It was giving away the deep despair and helplessness that I was enduring. My emotions were overruling any other, more rational thoughts from within. I immediately realised that the barrage of questions was the wrong thing to do. My brain fully comprehended that I should have remained calm, especially when dealing with a character such as Mark.

"No, Pete. I will talk to you when I see you in the morning. We can discuss the matter face to face. Plus the trip that you are heading on, OK?"

I agreed with the arrangements and sat overcome by sadness, enjoying a moment of solitude with the pain of my grief. My heart had sunk, waiting for the news I was expecting was like waiting for God. I knew however that I had to do what Mark had requested. I looked up at the starry sky, wondering, just wondering what was happening. Could the love of my life see what I was seeing? Could she feel what I was feeling? The worry was taking over my whole being, I felt that I was drowning in a sea of concern. Part of my soul had been severed, a missing portion of life, a vacant cavern carved out from within. I was aware that I had to remain fresh and alert for when the time came, no matter what the outcome was to be. I decided to get some sleep, while sinking to the deepest core of the earth with the weight that had been imposed upon my heart and mind.

I awoke with a sudden jolt, everything a blur in the total darkness of the night, the twisting pain from someone's knee was digging deep into the arch of my back, whilst I was being pulled by my hair. I struggled and rolled over to face my assailant for the second time in the last twelve hours. All I could think of was; why now? Why at this particular moment, at three o'clock in the morning was I being grabbed? Why tonight of all nights? I needed sleep. There were difficult and risky times ahead, no matter what the outcome, that I knew. Classic car runs for Mark could be a stressful way of supplementing one's income, this time that was the least of my worries.

After ten years of interrupted sleep and an irregular pattern of behaviour, I should have become fully prepared as such occurrences had gradually became the resting norm. Like the slow process of evolution itself, it had merged into everyday life. What was the reason for the interruption? Music. The CD player was wanted again. Who was it? This regular assailant was my severely autistic, ten year old daughter.

The Sunday afternoon inquisitors did not predict that activity within this house. The parents did not see themselves as the lucky ones when their little offspring were chatting to them. The harsh reality of a child with Autism still casts is ugly shadow across what, from the outside, is a mirage of affluent bliss. The life-changing shadow, that darkens deep over the simplest of activities, every single waking hour, of every single day. And waking hours with a hyperactive, autistic, ten year old, have saturated the market, their value plummeting like an economic theory.

It is a real shame that a beautiful, fun, mischievous little girl who has done no harm, is shaded from the world; its activities; experiences; learning; knowledge and conversations. The future ahead has been darkened, eliminating much of the definition, as well as the detail of the picture itself, switching off some of the lights of life, while substituting them with a dim glimmer. Not that Alice is not great and much adored, as she is. In fact, she is the inspiration of what I do to create as secure and protected a life for the future as is possible.

Not being able to understand, reason, react to basic responses to life, or communicate verbally, does come with frustrations and difficulties. Wrongly interpreted gestures, other unknown and often undiscovered happenings, or feelings, can often result in self-harming, most commonly by punching herself in the face. But there is a strong element of mischief, demonstrated by throwing things around and taking possession of items that one should not have. Frequently such behaviours are accompanied by a cheeky grin and an exit made as quickly as an Olympic competitor. While the acts themselves can often have the outcome of an item lost to the depth and powerful current of the river, or broken into fragments upon the floor.

I turned the CD player on for a while at low volume, the lively sound from the Mission speakers peeling out rock tracks such as; Status Quo, Bon Jovi, Queen, Meatloaf then a compilation of dance tracks; anything in fact that has a tune and a beat. Meanwhile, Alice sprinted up and down the safe, antique and breakable-free zone of the house, where all doors are locked, where the cupboards are fitted with catches to protect both our little mischief and our belongings from that potentially fatal, little grasp. I managed to doze off, sleeping intermittently between listening out for any signs of distress until the morning came, or shall I say, the conventional time for arising from one's dreams arrived.

To the outsider my morning attempts to style Alice's hair appeared to be a disaster, the indication of Dad attempting a style, but lacking all complete skill to create a slick, styled arrangement. In my view, I had been practising the art of styling Alice's hair for the last nine years and had reached a result that was different. I would even go as far as stating that my created styles were unique. Why not create a plat that has various stray hairs bushing out around it and offset on the head, like a grand master that has been hanging on a wall, through an earthquake? So a variant on the conventional style for Alice, it is.

The taxi and carer came to take Alice to school, cheerfully and reliably escorting their precious, unconventional cargo. I often wondered how other people and her surrounding environment appeared to Alice. What is her interpretation of the complex integration and interaction of sights, sounds, colours, movements, actions and behaviours? Not to mention the art of speech itself? Do those of us with more conventional traits, appear unconventional and strange? Is putting something down carefully upon the table, rather than throwing it over the fence, or at the floor to hear the sound of its fracture resonating through the house, a strange, illogical behaviour to Alice? Does she feel frustrated that we are all continuing our lives, day in day out, saturating them with pointless tasks, discussions, movements and emotions? Well this is something we are unlikely to ever have much insight of, yet alone comprehend.

In terms of conversation, is she really missing that much anyway? The meaningless small talk, empty throw-away comments and people attempting to; 'say the right thing' in their eyes, often not equating to the desired feedback in the eyes of the recipient. To complicate matters further, there are the exaggerations and lies, deception, the theatrical performances by those who have never taken to the stage, but who are truly star thespians. Then to make matters worse, there is the most confusing situation of all. Saying one thing, when in actual fact you mean something different, which may, at times, be the total opposite. Then again, who can comprehend the actions of another party, whether human being, or animal?

We may all follow the conventional expectations that are thrust upon us by society for the majority of the time, but what about the remainder; when behaviours step astray? What of the; murder, rape, abuse, acts of cruelty, not to mention some of the words and opinions stated? Surely, the logic and reasoning of many of these, is far less explainable than Alice's illogical logic?

I worried about my current situation, the despair of not knowing what was happening to the love of my life; whether she was in trouble, or pain. My hopes were becoming hinged on one person and the contacts that he had. This was the man that I was heading over to see.

Chapter 2

The Person in Control

I drove up the hill to enter Mark's drive. It was a new dwelling, standing strong, firm and controlling; resembling the character himself. The plot occupied a great elevated vantage point lying just outside of the town; protected by surrounding properties. It was a substantial house, but the exact opposite of my own residence. It was modern, with contemporary glass and rendered elevations punctuated by panels of cedar cladding. Pure, crisp lines, with no dressing up, or frills; all visible features were there for a purpose, with a job to do and not to add an additional dynamic.

The house was obscured along a narrow, gated, steep, tarmac track surrounded by hedging. At night, low level, coloured LED lighting lined the route. Concealment was clearly something that ranked highly within the owners mind. In this case, it was probably born out of necessity, rather than any particular, conscious desire to be hidden from view. The irony of it all was the system installed to identify all those who were approaching, by small, concealed, closed circuit television cameras that were camouflaged around the dwelling. Being able to view out and survey ones surroundings is one thing, but for people to look in and survey the surveyor is something totally different, yet all done in a manner so discrete, that to most, they would have gone unnoticed.

The meeting convened over tea, served within the substantial summer house, located at the top of the garden. The room was kitted out like a lounge, with only the timber walls and an expanse of glass panes to suggest that this was not a large, cosy, sitting room. Everything was there; from the cushions on the sofa, the deep rugs on the timber floor, to the modern entertainment system positioned in the corner.

Mark leant back, sighed and grinned, the bulk of his frame filling the chair. He was not a tall man, but wide and heavily built. His arms were of a girth greater than my legs and he emitted a sense of power and strength. Not just in his physical appearance, but also by his tough, controlling image, that he thrived upon, in a manner that oozed from every pore. Like his appearance, he was a hard man. He was clearly a force not to attempt to compete against, or dare to challenge in any way. His image preceded him throughout the region, as a person of control. The petty thief, the young trouble maker, and the hardened tough criminal, all treated him with the same utmost respect, placing him on a pedestal.

He was now nearing 60 so had decided to relax to some degree, let life pass by and was now accompanied with the means to enable this to happen, if that is what he really wanted. A collection of Italian sports cars were his hobby, not maintaining them, but driving them to the limit. Not on British roads of course, but Europe, as well as at track days at racing circuits around the country.

The extent of his decision to take life a little easier was, as yet, unknown. His competitive body building was over, but the strength and physique remained. How he originally achieved his image and retained it, I did not know. To gain the respect of anyone is hard enough, but to gain it in these circles, was no mean feat. To retain it for years, at all levels of the criminal hierarchy; that is something which is usually only ever achieved by the true gangster, or mafia. What elevated him to these dizzy heights was unknown to me and to remain that way. It was not a route that I had ever chosen to navigate with him, but one that I decided was probably best to steer well clear of; to conclude that ignorance *is* sometimes bliss.

It could have been violence and his insurmountable strength, but how does that remain? Maybe it was murder, but would someone stick up for a victim one day? Surely someone would compile evidence for the police? Maybe that cleverly using personality and image, to keep relationships ongoing within the various criminals and gangs of the underworld is a more plausible situation. It could only be pulled off successfully by someone very alert but diplomatic, who knew what was happening and how to stay in favour with them all. How to wear several hats with absolute discretion at all times, as well as being a great actor, to convincingly portray what was needed with everyone simultaneously.

One day there must be that deadly risk of being caught up in the crossfire, possibly even literally. This would be a task that was almost impossible, but if this was the approach, then it worked. In addition to the underworld, a controlling factor with the police would also be needed, preventing them from being a burden on everyday life.

There is a theory, that it is all no more than an act. That events are staged; with a hard, confident, image and persona portrayed without the slightest flicker of deviation, in every single situation. Circulate a few stories to reinforce the concrete and such conviction may never be doubted, or questioned.

Like the infamous Kray twins, people on the inside must be on the books in the police and at an appropriate level of the hierarchy to ensure the longevity of the success. This would be costly to maintain; requiring tight financial control like any efficient business, combined with an unofficial system of whom to pay, and more importantly; when. Anyway, yet again, the true methodology is something that we may never know.

"So how's everything going?"

I enquired, choosing to select a vague, indirect, method of questioning.

"Business is fine, if that is what you mean? The current recession is not totally a bad thing for me. We have fewer building sites to protect, but there are more small-time, thieving little bastards around. Usually trying their hand at something they know fuck all about. Not to mention, whose toes they are treading upon out there. They do not understand their chosen new career, who is who and whom to respect. The police catching hold of the bleeders would be for their own good, even though they will never have the sense to realise it."

I detected more than a little frustration in his voice and mannerism, that he was actually quite irritated by the opportunist, petty thief. I realised that after showing my despair on the telephone the night before, I had to remain cool. I had to exhibit the trait that was natural to Mark and one that I realised all too well, was something that he held in high regard. The trait did not come natural to me, yet alone when my soul mate was missing.

"You are taking it a bit easy now aren't you?" I enquired, keeping the questions at an elementary level.

"The business runs itself now, with staff and the kid taking control."

Now this was an interesting approach. How would the power, respect and image, be inherited if Mark was out of the scene? What was even more unusual, this was not a Son of the same build and stature starting to follow in Mark's footsteps, complete with the surrounding halo of power and force. *'The Kid'* he affectionately referred to, was his youngest offspring, he had two daughters, whom I had never met. She was destined to take up the security company helm, with construction sites, door staff and buildings to protect. She may be a force to be reckoned with, or blind everyone with her charm. Only time would tell.

"I have to go out soon pal, as something needs attending to. I have a small package to be picked up in France and a stone to be moved across Jersey. It is a bit different, this second one. You will need to pose as a buyer of the stone, then as the person selling it on. Any chances of booking in on a classic car run to Le Mans for the Classic 24? Then return the car as per the usual arrangements, before heading back via Jersey. Stay over a couple of days and make a break of it. Yeah, take a couple of days there in that place you two usually stay. I will get one of the staff to give you a call when you are on your way."

I looked across at Mark, my face probably revealing what I was thinking. It was just not the time for taking a few days away from home. He knew what I was thinking, reading people was a skill that his profession depended upon. He sat forward in his chair, smiled slightly but in a determined, rather than a soft way.

"Just do it. It will help. Trust me, it will. Are you taking the old one that does not lock?"

I got a definite feeling, as always, that questions were not questions at all in the true meaning of the word, but a masquerade of thoughts out loud, that are really clear instructions that simply must be followed. I had no option.

The approach usually suited me though, as we had developed a trust over the last few years, without getting too involved in the remaining areas of each other's life. To an extent, Mark's occupations may be almost unbearably intriguing in a brutal, hard, uncompromising, sort of way. It is apparent that consequences of actions are either given a low priority, or strategically planned around like any good business model, to maintain the risk levels within the appetite of a risk matrix. At the same time, I had made the decision that details were, in my circumstances, one to remain well clear of. The less I was aware of the better, choosing to ignore any involvement I had, and not to dwell upon what it was that I may be involved in.

"There is still no news by the way, but trust me; I am working on it. As soon as I find something out, which I assure you I will, you will know. You will never know just how much I appreciate what you are feeling. Right now, proceeding as normal is the key. Not showing any signs of distress provides the confidence that creates success."

I did trust him, I was sure that he would be doing all that he could. I knew it was right to play his game, follow his rules, this was his profession. I had to ignore my frantic, irrational, thoughts and emotional attachment. This was something that did not apply to Mark. It was not the love of his life that was missing, maybe as a result of some criminal act. If Mark said that it would help, I had to proceed on that basis, convincing myself that he was correct. For all I knew, there may be some relevance to the chain of events.

"Mark; I am doing this, but it does not feel like the right time. It is not my priority in life. You know where that lies; with my heart. Please do what you can. Please. Promise you will keep me informed of any news. She would not leave like this of her own free will. She simply would not do it. Keep me in the loop damn it."

I would love to have elaborated further, placed greater emphasis on what I was feeling inside. I knew that with Mark it would be counter-productive, so controlled my soul, holding in the ever expanding panic. I realised he knew that already, the look on my face would not have been disguised by any mask. Words were only adding to the obvious. He smiled sympathetically, lips firmly clenched and accompanied by a knowing nod.

On the sombre note we said our farewells, as I returned home to investigate the routes, itinerary and the all-important preparation of the car. The last thing that we wanted was for the car to have a tantrum at the wrong moment. Keeping as per our schedule would be an important factor and the car to be taken was the oldest; the 1958 Austin Healey Sprite Mk I finished in Cherry Red, with red interior and hood. A detachable white hardtop was fitted for the winter, or shall we say, the worst moments of the British climate; as since when has winter been the capsule of the poor weather.

The Frogeye was, on the face of it, an unusual choice, even by the standards of my collection, for the completion of a 500 mile trip to France. Down to the Channel Tunnel, then theoretically tour South-West across France to Le Mans. It has headlights set in bulges in the bonnet, surmounting a cheeky looking radiator grill that appears to grin. The hood is removable, so are the side screens rather than winding windows.

No creature comforts had been designed into the model when new, even by 1958 standards, yet alone the expectations of customers today. A basic, cheap, sports car with no frills was the original concept of the design. The engine was 948cc, the gearbox had no synchromesh to first gear, no door locks were fitted and external door handles were even conspicuous by their absence. Entry through the small door was gained by reaching over the door with the roof off, or by putting ones arm through the sliding side screens, feeling around to release the door catch within the car itself. No door trim panels here, not even an opening boot lid. The luggage compartment was accessed from within the car, open behind the two seats. What made up for all of this however, was the nimble handling, twitchy steering, the soundtrack played by the exhaust, the driving experience and character, of human and machine becoming one. It was some of these attributes however, that made the car the ideal choice for the task ahead and what Mark had in mind.

I was well aware that if I wanted a little like-minded company along the route, it was readily available, someone to follow along the French stretch of the journey, navigating abroad while driving on the right-hand side of the road, in an area totally unfamiliar. Travelling as a group also provided a far better alibi if anything did not proceed to plan.

There was a club for the little cars, each year a few members from around the country, who were far more enthusiastic about the classic car racing scene than I, would make the pilgrimage to Le Mans.

The race itself was not one 24 hour long race, but a series of classic car races, staged on the famous circuit over a 24 hour period, one of the few places that night racing could be experienced. Calls were made, arrangements discussed, clothes packed and the car prepared. A few spares for the car were packed away within the dark confines of the boot, with a collection of tools, wrapped in protective cloth for the long journey ahead. I took a few old ignition parts, too, which I had removed, finding them faulty during a breakdown a couple of years ago.

All that now remained was to give Alice a fond farewell, prior to the early-hours departure for the south coast. She was going to be well looked after for the next few days. A former teacher at her special school for autistic children now worked for us, which was ideal for school holidays and business trips. She was well experienced with autistic children, having several years' experience working at autistic special schools, both here and in her native Germany. She was around thirty-five, short but sturdy for her size, with dark hair. She was physically fit, quick and strong, previously spending many years rowing competitively as a hobby, having had the commitment and focus to train every day. This was a hidden asset, with the speed and determination that Alice can frequently display when darting towards something that catches her observant eyes.

The commitment exhibited in the tough, competitive world, was something that had transformed well into this role, demonstrating reliability that would be hard to match. Such skill having proved to be an asset, one that would never have sprung to mind when considering the attributes of any potential applicants for the role. Any time she was required, she would be there. The role also offered flexibility, so was a match for both parties, any rowing events and training programmes that she wanted to attend, were usually easy to accommodate. With the River Trent outside the perimeter wall, a little hands-on experience could also be undertaken at the start, or end of work.

The only downside to the smiley character, was that sometimes conversations took a little longer than expected. Not only due to the personality that made chatting easy, but because by her own admission, she thought in her native German, prior to translating to discuss a topic in English. To me, who had never had any aptitude for languages, this was a skill that could never be conceived. Like the German meaning of her name; Antonie had become priceless.

On this occasion, my mind was turned upside down, a few days away was not what I wanted. I had to continue, concealing all within, so that to the outside world no change was evident. I had to focus, no matter what I was feeling inside. It was the approach that Mark had requested. All that remained was for me to convince myself that it would; 'create the confidence that creates success'. That it would be material to finding the missing love of my life. That it would ensure her safety. Any doubts had to be rejected; what help would worrying be anyway? I had no other option.

It was to be a stressful, tough battle; I knew that, no matter what the outcome was to be. The pressure inside was building, the frustration expanding within my mind, not helped by a loss of appetite and increased restlessness. I wanted to jump up, to run, to shout, and to lash-out; but could not establish where, or at what. I had to fight my instinct and strong desire while not becoming critically unstable.

Chapter 3

The Old Day Job

It was a great early morning start for the classic sports car enthusiast; warm, dry and dark but still, ideal conditions for roofless driving along twisting, quiet, country lanes heading for the A1. The sweet scent of the summer flowering plants perfumed the atmosphere. The bird song gathered in volume as the day dawned. The intensity of the surroundings became stronger, as the muted, pastel colours became more vivid and true. As soon as I increased speed, the breeze increased its power and the sense of unity with the machine became more vivid. Eventually the sounds of nature became overpowered, being replaced by the exhaust note; an equally as attractive quality.

I joined the A1 for the long journey south, with few cars, but many goods vehicles travelling on the quieter roads of the early hours. This is where even when driving a classic, there is a degree of sameness and monotony along the relatively straight lanes stretching into the distance and beyond.

So how did I get here? Not the journey this morning, or the evolution of life itself, but why was I doing this? Why now? How did I come to live my current lifestyle, to be the person who resides in that place, doing what the person who lives there does each day? How did all this come about? Why was the love of my life missing? The answer to a few of the questions that the Sunday afternoon inquisitor would wish to source a response to were a little more dramatic than they might imagine.

A little over eleven years ago, my lifestyle was conventional. Conventional job as a Surveyor for a residential property developer, conventional company car, the usual four bedroom detached house and of course, the usual rush hour trips to and from the office. Not that there is any rushing in or out of the modern, bland, characterless Business Park at the edge of any city, or large town in the country. They are always populated with uniform, regimented offices, cloaked with different cladding or fenestration to create a different type of rectangular box. Once within, people work long hours in air-conditioned germ factories with no opening windows. Of course, parking cars in such locations is an art form in itself. How to arrange as many cars, in as fewer spaces as possible, resulting in chunks of the working day being spent shuffling them about like different suits in a well handled pack.

The job was something that I found interesting; property development but something that I had drifted towards after completing a surveying degree. At the time of my graduation the conventional route to work for a surveying and valuation practise was, at best, difficult as the property market was depressed, itself depressing those who worked within the industry. General practice surveyors were merging. Well, merging was not the word. Long established local practices, dating from the nineteenth century were being absorbed by London practises, trying to grasp clients and work around the country, in it for the short-term client addition to the database. Playing for numbers was the game, not ongoing, long-term, stable foundations for future business. This was evaporating long established names to claim the figures, changing the profession for good, but not for the better.

For me, hard work from early to late was expected, with rewards that did not match the effort applied, unless of course, you were the type of person who did the minimum that you could get away with. For some success was to be judged on chatting to the Directors, the Managing Director and Senior Shareholders. Talking about some executive holiday, or time spent travelling in ones younger years, rather than applying oneself to hard work and effort for a source of reward. Of course, this was something that I was unaware of at the time. My misconception was that effort, time spent working constructively, and generating quality opportunities would be something that created reward. Thinking that identifying land and assembling the difficult deals that were to create a hefty margin or profit, should stand one in good stead.

I developed a niche in piecing together the more complex sites, where past uses had left the land contaminated, or were difficult to develop due to the proximity of services, cables, or other abnormal items. As long as all of the abnormal elements were known, costs identified, risks assessed and the site itself was negotiated hard, to purchase at a cautious level, this type of site could be a gold mine in the returns for the investment made. They do say; where there is muck there is brass, and Brownfield property development is a prime example. Great returns could be achieved from the sale of the right product, in the right location. All of this however takes knowledge, skill, experience and judgement but also knowing when to stop. The various permutations of products that could be placed upon the said land, were then the key to unlock the most profitable return. For over six years, my dedication was applied to the role, with the thought process of 'work' not switched off when the clock struck five, or the midnight hour turned to become a Saturday morning. I was certainly value for money when compared with someone who has a toggle switch mind that diverts all thought and intent into pleasure, on the strike of the clock.

I had been told that reward in the form of Directorship was an imminent arrival for me. I worked harder, pushed harder, achieved more, results escalated and targets were smashed. There was one condition however, the securing of a key parcel of prime development land with river frontage. It was to become the new hub of the town, to embrace the trendy professionals and the young within a collection of café bars. The office space and high quality apartments were to survey the cult destination from above, adding value to accompany the facade of fashion below. The parking was to be under ground, beneath an epicentre of vibrant activity, all focussed around a water feature. This was to become the place to be. The image was created, professionals working lunches by day, the glamorous life for the trend setters by night. The plan was to be implemented, to attract business by day and night from the surrounding region, to maximise the sense of place, vibrancy, hours of activity and with it profitability.

There was one outstanding barrier to overcome, to be removed and relocated; the scrap yard occupying the river frontage site. Without this acquisition, what appeal and image could the development ever offer and what profit could be liberated? River frontage was not the only key, but the removal of the bad neighbour itself, to allow the novel to proceed as it was written. All that stood in my way to the dream job was the acquisition of the yard, owned by one; Noel Harrington.

This was the ace of my deck. Not just the opportunity for the directorship, but my contact with the scrap yard owner himself. The well-established yard was owned by a man, well into his seventies whom I had previous dealings with in the past as a customer. As a classic car fan he had been a source of parts for cars over the years. The yard was not just a final resting place for accident damaged and ageing cars that were beyond their economic life, but also the home of a collection of salvaged classic cars. Some would be purchased to be lovingly restored by a future owner, but some that were sadly beyond the point of no return, being only suitable as parts. Noel Harrington was well known as a minefield of unpredictability and eccentricity. His business dealings, customer care, moods and whole approach to life, would swirl around to change direction quicker than a whirlwind, accompanied by the unpredictability, uncertainty, chaos and potential damage of all that lay in his path. Yet if he got on with you, there could be no better friend; just needing a little careful handling with protective gloves when the prickly need arose. Thought by some as eccentric, others as cantankerous and annoying, well to me, he was a warm, welcoming individual most of the time. He just lacked any desire to pretend to be something that he was not. You received what he wanted to give at that moment in time, like it, or not. With his vast knowledge of older cars and their components he had a great deal to give, a one man website of information, but requiring multiple passwords to access.

He knew the worth of the site that he had to offer and the potential to make, or break the scheme. He also knew that the Local Authority wanted him out and that Compulsory Purchase was an option. There were therefore three approaches to the assembly of this final parcel.

The first being Compulsory Purchase through the official channels, while being offered suitable alternative accommodation, which for a bad neighbour use such as a scrap yard, was hard to find. Objections from nearby landowners would be rife, along with the environmental implications of the land use.

The second option was the use of Compulsory Purchase powers to buy his site based on his turnover, more costly, but negating the need to find the alternative site. Since the development proposal had become known to him, his turnover had increased one hundred fold. He was no busier, but his previous accounts that had illustrated a struggle to cover costs, had miraculously changed over the last two years, to generate an extremely healthy profit, which would question the economics of any purchase through this route.

These two options would also have one major difficulty; speed. Compulsory Purchase could often take two years to resolve. By the time this had occurred, the option to purchase some of the other parcels of land that we held, would have expired. At the same time, any crack in the proposal would gradually erode into a deep chasm during the process. The scheme would become more public, increasing the risk of rival developers, or speculators making the purchase of key landholdings to block our path, creating a ransom, playing an expensive game of noughts and crosses.

The third option was for me to do a deal, to purchase the site direct from Noel. This way the land could be acquired in a timely manner with all factors remaining within our control. For me, this was the way it just had to be.

"What's occurring with the land assembly for The Hub? The Options expire in a month and we need to purchase."

Dean Knowles; the Managing Director had walked up to my desk, doing his rounds, mingling with the troops, an ideal camouflage for surveying what the young, female pool of staff were wearing, sorry, doing. After all, someone may have made the mistake in falling for his charms, his outward friendliness, or have attended work wearing something that illustrated a degree of the female form. Maybe a top was a little lower cut than usual, a skirt a little shorter, trousers a little tighter, or even a gap of tattooed flesh revealed above some curved shape when bending down to the photocopier. Maybe it was just showing interest in his staff, combined with adding a little motivation by being exposed on the open-plan office floor, rather than looking for a little exposure. Then again, I had known him for a good few years and realised he was not someone who was likely to ever change.

Dean was fairly tall, thin, with dark hair greying on his approach to his half-century. His most recent appointments and actions were evidencing the inner panic he was experiencing in achieving the milestone, he was someone that found it hard to be politically correct in the modern office, being more comfortable when being viewed as one of the lads. He knew where I was with the deal, we had spoken at length earlier in the week and should have known my methods of progressing schemes, even before the ultimate incentive that he had introduced.

"It is all in hand Dean. The land to be acquired has security arranged to prevent any unwanted campers, or any materials of value being removed. I am using THE person for the job, the person that everyone in the region will take notice of, Noel Harrington knows him well too."

"Mark Daniels! You are dealing with Mark, be careful of that one, if you do not come in one morning I will visit you in the hospital. Do you want flowers, or donations at your funeral?"

Dean's jokey manner, immediately making light of the reputation Mark had with almost everyone who knew of him. This was a reaction that most people tended to show, although I personally had no issues with him.

Protection for sites that had been purchased was a necessity. There was the issue of people moving onto the site, squatting, or camping, plus the removal of potentially valuable scrap that would help to off-set the demolition costs, the most common being the high value trade of copper, almost a currency in itself. In addition there was the liability that goes with being the building owner and keeping it secure. The irony that a person gaining access to our land, can have an accident on a dangerous metal spike, then try to take legal action against us, when they should not have been intruding on our property in the first place.

"It is interesting that those two know each other." I commented. "Mark and his reputation, the activity that people say he is up to, whether it is fiction or not, and a scrap yard owner. Then again, there is money in it as we know. If you wanted to steal a load of scrap, then why not make life easy and break in to a scrap yard and sell it to another."

Dean looked around. "And how is the old man going, good luck with that one. I hope he is not messing us about, no pressure to deliver of course!"

"I am seeing him tonight, he invited me to his house to go through the detail in quieter surroundings, I will know what the situation is one way or another by the morning."

Scott interrupted as usual to lick Dean's shoes, sorry, I mean to talk about nothing, holidays, something that he had done last night, or heard on the Radio during the monotonous drive to the office. Dean's attention left me to converse about nothing, for some reason there was some form of bond between them, even though they had never liked each other since Scott joined the company. Scott was a good 'jobs worth', with everything being black, or white, strictly corporate and by the rules. There is nothing wrong with that in itself, if the rules made sense in the first place, but often here, like many places, they did not. Dean had been recently promoted to Managing Director. He was not a rules person, he was a negotiator, a deal closer, that role and strict rules do not match. To succeed at that role, flexibility is needed and to be fair, for all of his faults, he was talented at it. The promotion of Dean had changed Scott's attitude towards him, he now mattered to Scott. Anyway, the conversation with me had come to an abrupt end, I was sure the conversation about nothing would as well, as soon as someone young and more aesthetically pleasing appeared. After all, it was summer, so a little exposure may soon enter the radar.

I was off to visit Noel Harrington and I have to say, I wondered what his place would be like. I knew where he lived, but had never visited him at home. In fact, I had never seen him out of his overalls and part covered in oil, grease and dirt from the yard. I approached his house at the edge of a quiet village and turned into his overgrown drive. It was a detached Georgian house of red brick, with a centrally mounted, uniform door to the front, located close to the road. A shallow front garden, with pretty bedding plants brightened up what looked quite dull, dank and green. The drive twisted to the rear of the house, once stoned, now overgrown with grass, weeds and moss.

I parked my car next to his truck. Various old barns and stables clearly housed the overspill of items from the yard. Items that had an interest level to Noel just too great to be left to rot in the scrap yard. Here they had a quieter, more respectful resting place. I wondered if this was all his intentional personal collection, or simply partly long lost, forgotten items, placed there over the years while awaiting transfer to the yard. Noel appeared, having heard the clatter of the company Audi diesel engine enter the courtyard. He came from one of the old barns near the fields behind the house. It looked as if the house once had been the centre of a farm, with various out buildings surrounding the rear rather than a conventional garden. An old mill building, almost derelict, stood to the side of the house, with a sadly rusting traction engine parked to the fore, its sorry sight still not detracting from the size and power of this great piece of engineering.

Noel's small, slightly tubby figure approached, his grey hair covered with a flat cap and wearing navy blue overalls. Not the dirty, grease stained ones from the yard, but clean ones to compliment his clean hands and face. I got a distinct impression with how at home he was in his choice of garment, that this may well be his Sunday best, a clean pair, worn especially when he was expecting a visitor. I could not help wondering if he ever wore anything else? We exchanged pleasantries and I followed him into the house, armed with my brief case that was as important to me, as the old, tatty one carried by the Chancellor of the Exchequer on Budget day. Mine was crisp, clean in black leather and contained all that was needed to close a deal, subject to the final legal contracts being prepared. I could not help but feel slightly nervous as to what lay ahead and what the outcome of this pleasant summer evening was to be.

"Come in and sit down, what will you drink?"

Noel asked, while turning around to place two whisky glasses and a bottle of whiskey on the coffee table in the lounge. It was a question that was evidently already answered before I uttered a word in reply, but one that suited my taste and I believe that he somehow already knew that.

"That will be lovely, thank you. We share the same taste." I said whilst removing the plans, surveys and appraisals of the scheme from my case.

"Now look, straight to the point, that's me, it's how I was brought up, that's how I am. I have had the place valued and I want two million, not a penny less. It is worth it to you lot. I know it is not big, but it is the best spot, and there is no point building around me. My yard is as noisy, dirty and smelly as I want to make it. That'll put off all the bloody dressed up toffs from visiting your fancy scheme."

Noel turned around to face me as I considered the figure; I was pleased with his direct approach.

I knew the appraisals and figures for the scheme. The projected construction and contamination remediation costs, margins, estimated end capital value and projected rental incomes. I was relieved and grew gradually excited, feeling the adrenalin rush of hoping to close the deal. I could in actual fact have increased by an additional £350,000 if I had needed. I decided not to negotiate, but to agree on a Subject to Contract basis as I realised that if old Mr Harrington said two, he meant two and not a penny under.

"We have a deal." I said, relieved, calmly containing my delight.

"It's not that I want the money you know, I'm late seventies now and The Wife died eight years ago, so I have no plans for it. I have plenty to keep me going until I go, although I have lost loads of it to the tax man, bloody thief. Since you lot have been sniffing around at the yard, it has been a case of recording everything we could. I just want out of all of this, it's not what it was. Green this, green that, green the bloody other. Grass is green, trees are green, industrial products, well, and they simply are not. Recycling huh! Recycled everything, recycled bloody toilet tissue my arse. I have had enough of all the environmental controls and regulations crap. If it was rubbish and we could burn it, we used to burn it and I'm still here. I'm a scrap man, always was, always will be. I started out at fifteen you know, collecting any old metal and built up from there. My father was into horses and carts for all types of things, deliveries, ploughing, to funerals, but to me they were just a way of getting the scrap. I had one bolt on me once and lost half me lead in the River Trent. After that, I got a lorry as soon as I could afford one. Mmmm might buy me self a new pickup. My Grandson can have the rest."

"What are you going to do with your time and the classics?" This was a question that given my interest, I could not resist asking.

"Well, start to restore old Bessy me traction engine out there, I have collected parts and have a lathe set up in the workshop. As for the cars, I will bring the ones that are true classics here for spares, or for restoration; I'm quite looking forward to it."

So was I, but for very different reasons. The whisky diminished as the conversations went on and I started to forget about the job, but look around the room. It was cluttered with antiques, paintings and dust. Amongst the lounge furniture was part of an engine, laid out on old newspaper, acting as a centrepiece to the carpet. The wallpaper was peeling and I could not miss that the kitchen was well past its best. All the rooms I had seen had been painted dingy, dull shades, probably created from various part cans mixed together. The paint and items around the room reduced the Georgian grandeur, only being partially compensated by the high ceilings and large windows with their peeling paint.

"I will tell Mark Daniels what we have agreed. He will keep his eye on the place. We have an arrangement, a sort of mutual exchange, so he does not charge.

I had a reputation a bit like his once, did a bit of boxing when I was a lad and only one person ever tried to cross us, my brother and I. It was the late '60's and this bloke who worked for me was on the take, big time. I trusted him you know, that was the worst thing, he looked after the place for years when I was not around. He'd been siphoning things off and selling them, letting things go to people and pocketing the cash. Year after year he had been doing it. My brother caught him when I was out, then started asking around to get the full story like. I still have not got over the betrayal now, I said to myself then; I would never let anyone get away with it and I still feel the same now. I sent him up to my brothers' farm, to pick up an old irrigation pump one evening. Then we waited for him. We gave him a right pasting, never saw him again. The police came a week later, thought we had crushed a car with him in the boot. Kicked up a right stink it did. As if we would have been so stupid, he deserved it alright. He deserved worse, but leave him in a car in the yard, no way. I can think of better ways, pigs eat the lot you know, there would be nothing left. Anyway, wherever he went, it was away from here."

I could not help but feel as if I had received a slight warning as I bid my farewells. He had clearly been amused by the later parts of his tale. This also coupled with his friendship of the infamous Mark Daniels. I walked to the car as Noel approached.

"When will they do the barns?" he queried. I turned and looked at him slightly puzzled, taken aback by this sudden, random, question that appeared as if it had travelled down with the beams of moonlight that illuminated the drive.

"Sorry, I'm not with you Nocl?"

"Me barns here." He nodded across at the structures near the house.

"They need to re-roof them sharpish to get them watertight before buying the yard. The roof is half off one after the winds last October. Until your company has done that, I can't get the classic cars down here, without them out, I cannot wrap the yard up and sell it to yer."

I agreed we would sort it, after all, making them water tight was not such a big job, and I did have the £350,000 to fall back on. On my way home, my feeling of delight was slightly tempered by the thought of any new, added conditions travelling down in the rays of the morning sunlight.

Chapter 4

The End of Normality

I was now well down the A1, the traffic getting busier, a combination of the time of day and the proximity to London, the faster, bustling end of the country. The monotony was only broken by a trio of E-Type Jaguars passing by, waving as they went, the sound of their V12 engines burbling along, effortless even at speed. Without a doubt they were also heading for Le Mans. I thought back again to the end of my previous lifestyle and the new beginning that was created. I had become involved in a whole new set of circumstances, in a situation that I never could have imagined. Not just Alice and her autism, or the life-long changes that were Siamese with her condition, but the earlier changes to my life. From Surveyor for a developer through to what I do now and the dramatic, sudden way that it came about.

***

The morning came I arrived in the office early to instruct our solicitor. All was going to plan. Dean Knowles walked in the building, a little late as usual, but still eager for a news update. I filled him in with the details of the night before, including Noels final wish regarding the improvements to the barns.

"Well done, well done that man. Get the barns priced up and as soon as we are in contract, get it carried out. It is the Board Meeting in three weeks so it would be good to have everything in place for then. I have to appoint the new Director at the Annual General Meeting that same evening following on from Board, too."

Minutes merged into hours, late nights merged into early mornings, days into nights, weekdays into weekends and a bank holiday into the working week; all to ensure that there was nothing to stop the deal. Everything was in place and contracts were exchanged. I spent most of the time out of the office, liaising with the Solicitor, Noel Harrington, the Architect, Quantity Surveyor and Engineer. Every single day became one long meeting, every evening, night and weekend being the time to catch up and progress on paper and laptop.

The day of the Board meeting arrived. It was a day that I had been looking forward to for months, like an excited child waiting for Christmas to eventually arrive and much wanted gifts to be revealed. After all I had been promised the Directorship in return for what I had now delivered. I was in the office early, eager of what the day ahead was to bring. Dean and Scott walked over to my desk, a slightly unexpected form of greeting, not anticipating them to be together, especially before mid-morning. They both displayed smiles all the same. They did however have a sense of togetherness and unity, an unusual quality for the combination that has never been known to get along. They placed themselves on the chairs in front of the desk, still smiling, quietly and calmly Dean began to talk.

"You did a great job on the scrap yard and land assembly of the other sites, now we have to deliver the scheme. Rather than buying new land we have the deal to bring forward and construct. I know what you were promised in the past, this is a big deal and it is down to you. You have secured the largest scheme we have done and hopefully it will generate our greatest return, making us the main player in the region and a key player in the wider market. For that reason we must focus on delivery, so I am appointing a new Director."

Dean and Scott both sat back.

I could not understand the reason for the audience and waited with anticipation and a touch of confusion for what was to follow. I did not have to wait for long before Dean ended my confusion.

"I am sorry that it has to be this way, but Scott is to be made the new Director. He is to look after the delivery of the scheme and you can assist him having full knowledge of the deal."

My heart sank, plummeting to the darkest depths of the ocean. I could not believe what Dean had said. I sat back in my chair attempting to comprehend what my brain was filtering and analysing. After all that I had put in, the hours, week in, week out, all I had missed in my own life, all for the company. The reward promised not coming into fruition, was one thing. The fact that Scott had been rewarded for nothing apart from creeping was something else. This was something that was beyond my comprehension, beyond my belief, the twist of the knife was felt, with the serrated edge severing and tearing the flesh of the already inflicted wound. Rather than a simple, clean cut that would heal with time, this twisting, tearing, ripping of flesh would leave a scar for life. The whole concept of hard work and results bringing just reward had disappeared into the distance, through a thick, swirling dense fog. It was lost at sea forever within the Bermuda Triangle of thoughts. This belief had now gone and one that would never return.

I attended the presentation and Board Meeting later in the day, not wanting to be at the office, but not sinking to their lower level, remaining professional. It was however the last place that I wanted to be right now. I felt frustrated and restless, wanting to get out into the country and have a good quick, long walk, time to think, time to dream, time to breath in the fresh country air, absorbing the sights and smells that differed so greatly from the world of work. The energy used would soak up my frustrations, the tiredness would set in as the sponge became saturated and tame the restless feeling of wanting to run outside.

Colleagues were shocked and could not understand the decision so they tried to form a logical reason. The main theory was wondering if Scott had something over Dean. Had he found something out about him either in, or outside of the office? Had he suggested using something against him? Was there another more sinister hidden agenda, or pact between them to explain this sudden merger of enemies? While I had been out finalising the deal, the two had become unusually close, something that had never been demonstrated before, in fact, prior contact was often treated with contempt.

Following the meeting Scott approached, his small, rounded figure was heading in my direction. He came up to my desk and spoke. His fake cultured accent in complete contrast from his true roots. I wondered what in these circumstances he was going to say. Obviously with his new found power, it would be great words of wisdom that only a Director could suggest.

"There is one thing I want to change on The Hub, it is a great deal, well done and I will enjoy having it on site with you. The money fine, the contract is exchanged, but waterproofing a barn, that is a different story, I know we have the quotations and it is all set to be done next week, but it is hassle. Just too much hassle. Let the old boy get his own builder in with his millions. If we had to pay for it due to the contract fine, but let him sort it himself. Try it on first though see if we can get out of it first."

Great! I thought as I said goodnight, a few short hours in to the role and he is meddling in the deal. If it had been early on in the negotiations then fine, but not now, not at this stage when it was agreed with Dean. I knew that this change of approach with Noel was going to go down like a lead balloon, well, far worse as at least with the afore-mentioned it had scrap value.

I left for home, having experienced something worse than any bad day at the office. Noel Harrington was someone to visit in the morning. Right now I had an important appointment, one that would last a few hours, hopefully distracting my frantic thoughts. It was to be nothing other than a meeting with the drinks cabinet and my old car in the garage. My 1975 MG Midget 1500 stood in the garage, its rare tundra paintwork lightly rusting and currently not running on the road. It was supposed to be my hobby; the restoration, but all spare time recently had been spent working in complete isolation from any hobby, friend, family or indeed, the outside world. Planet work had been all that existed, from now on it was to be considered as a cell, where I would be a captive prisoner, held against my will. I tried to start the car, but the whirring, spinning noise of a stuck starter motor prevented it bursting into life. Its failure to run had occurred more and more frequently over the last few months, stripping the aforementioned component had gained nothing, apart from limited revival. A replacement it was to be.

I arrived at the scrap yard early in the morning, intending to get the task over with. I was not looking forward to breaking the news to Noel. As soon as I arrived, I said what I had to say, keeping it strictly to the point, explaining it was the decision of the new Director and what had happened. He was not happy, the expression on his face had changed, it become older and almost fierce, his eyes hardening. He realised it was now out of my control and I was not personally rescinding on the offer.

"I have no problem with you, but with that new Director of yours I do. It's not the money, not arranging the repair, just the bloody cheek of the bastard to try this on, especially now at this stage. He wants stringing up by the balls for this. How are you now he has got the fancy new job and car no doubt?"

"I'm fine, nothing I can do about it, what's done is done. I'll find a new opportunity elsewhere when one arrives."

"Stop being so bloody professional, you are obviously pissed off after what you put into that place."

"To make matters worse, the starter motor gave up last night, too. Small thing I know but just to further decorate the icing on the cake."

"Call back at three, I will have a letter for you to take to the two Pratts and I'll dig out a new starter motor as well."

I left, not believing how understanding Noel Harrington had been, but well aware of the hard, steely look in his blue eyes. It was a look of hatred deep down, not at me, but at the decision that had been made. He had made it crystal clear in the past that he did not like being betrayed, or people deviating from their word.

Chapter 5

The Start of Abnormality

I returned home to spend a little time on the car, despite my usual commitment and professionalism I could justify clawing a little time back under these circumstances. Later on, actions may be required as a result of this letter, which of course, could go on late. Besides, my usual high level of self-motivation had taken a tumble by the recent happenings. It had slid down uncontrollably, falling deeper and deeper, gaining velocity, impact and picking up small niggles along the route. The result was the creation of a full scale avalanche, who knows what was lying in its path and when the calm, stillness would return to the summit.

I washed and changed, then headed off back to Noel's yard. I parked in front of the port-a-cabin which formed the office, with the old Victorian warehouse standing proudly at the rear. It was redbrick, with a slate roof, structurally sound, but tatty, having suffered from years of neglect and abuse. The three storey building had high floor to ceiling heights, standing far higher than its floor levels would suggest. The elevation facing the river soaked up water like a sponge. Following periods of heavy rain, the river would widen and rise up the bank to make contact with the brick, lapping up the building itself. The thick walls gradually deteriorating over the years, no doubt since it was first constructed. Its latest function was to become its final role to play in the long history.

In a matter of weeks, the old warehouse would be carefully destroyed by a demolition team, keen to save any material of salvage value. It had been modified in the 1960's, losing much of the buildings character and historic value, so was not considered worthy of retention. If the proposed development was not to be a focus for the town, a new centre for the business and trendy communities, then the historic value may have been more highly regarded by the Local Authority. They wanted to create a sustainable town and were focused on the economic development of the settlement that The Hub would bring. The final days were rapidly passing by before its historic sacrifice to The Hub. For now however, it was used for the storage of the better cars and parts that were removed from them; all gradually being examined, sorted and relocated. This was no mean feat; I believed that only Noel with his encyclopaedia-like mind for car parts would have any chance in identifying the items. They were all catalogued all right, but not on computer, not even on paper, but in his ageing mind.

Noel said nothing, he looked serious as he handed me a letter marked; 'Private and Confidential' the addressee being the name of Dean Knowles.

"Granddad, Granddad when are you going to buy me that new game you promised? I have been really good helping and will show you how to play it tonight."

"I'm busy at the moment, Josh, but maybe later."

"But, Granddad, you promised. You said that if I was good when I came to stay with you, I could have a new game. We could play together."

We both turned to face Josh, a small boy probably about eight years of age, casually dressed in what were, I am sure, clean clothes on his arrival to stay with Granddad earlier in the day. Now, though, he had clearly spent a few hours in the scrap yard, playing in the cars and running through the warehouse amongst the dirt, oil and grease. The evidence of his activities clearly displayed for all to see. It was apparent that he had been having a great time, but was not modelling the most appropriate attire for his games and exploration. The little blond figure, with blue eyes ran to an old, rusting brown lorry lurking in the corner of the yard. He quickly climbed up, squeezing himself through the partially opened door to a position behind the steering wheel. Pretending to drive, his figure was dwarfed by the size of the lorry, with his head just projecting above the wheel.

Noel turned and smiled; "I did promise him, but with the events of today I have not had chance to take him across town. He wants a new game from that store over at the edge of the business park opposite your offices. He's a good lad, into everything and getting quicker by the day, but he loves to come here then return to mine to stay over. I always get in trouble with the daughter-in-law like. She likes him nicely groomed and dressed. Every time he comes to me, be it here, or at home, he ends up in the old cars and gets greased up. Apparently last time he came his clothes were ruined. Don't see that a few oil stains matter myself, as long as he is having fun. I meant to get him a small set of overalls, but I am having trouble with his size. I don't suppose ... no, no, too much to ask, you have enough on at the moment."

"I can take him when I drop the letter off if you want? I can park in the office, assuming I can find a space at this time, and walk across to that game store, whatever it is called. It is only the other side of the main road backing onto the town. It would save you leaving here and parking up in town. I have to admit, I know nothing about gaming though, so I would not know what to get."

"If you are sure it is no trouble? I bet there will be a visitor space free under the office, there always has been when I have visited. He knows what he wants, in fact, I am sure he will teach you a thing or two about them. I have that to look forward to tonight. He does love classic cars, though, so I'm sure he will love to hear about your MG, he's a good lad so he will be no bother."

"No problem, I will enjoy it. A little different company will be good, take my mind off work for a while."

"Just one thing you must promise to do, call me from your mobile when you get inside the store. I want to know what game he wants, make sure it is suitable like, doesn't matter how much it is, as long as it is one that's right for his age. Go and tell him, just open your boot first and I'll put a new starter motor in it for you while you fetch him, it's on me."

I opened the boot, placed the letter; an A4 sized envelope that was thick enough to contain a legal document, or plans of the yard on to the front passenger seat, then headed over to the lorry.

"I'm a lorry driver picking up loads of scrap for Granddad," he said peering down from the white and brown cab.

Josh was sitting at the steering wheel of the lorry, amongst a jungle of tangled stray wires from the wiring loom where switches had been removed and sold. The grey stripped upholstery was torn and dirty, the foam squab exposed. Shreds of the headlining dangled above his head like the branches of a Weeping Willow Tree.

"You are doing a great job, now about that game you want, shall I take you to get it while Granddad finishes off here?"

"Will you? Will you please? I want this new good one where..."

Josh sprang into action, revealing for the first time the turn of speed that Noel had referred to. Jumping down from the cab, he was still talking about the game as his words became lost running towards his Granddad. He was just coming out of the old warehouse, within his arms was the heavy new starter motor, he placed it in the boot and closed the lid.

“Best get you cleaned up first. If it gets back to your mum that you have gone into town in this mess your Granddad will be in big trouble, huge trouble, and gigantic trouble!”

The ‘cleaned up’ version of Josh climbed into the back of the car. His hands and face were now basically clean, but grubby marks still prevailed on his clothes from his fun on the yard. He was desperately trying to win the battle with his excitement on the thought of the new game, but clearly not going to receive a medal to commemorate any victory.

“Josh be good. Now just remember, drop the letter off first so they can read it, and then call me when you have walked across to the shop.” Noel pushed a few crumpled notes into my hand through the window to be spent in the eagerly awaited store.

I had received my orders, this was worse than being at work, and then again, I was. Entertaining an eight year old was to me, far harder and more worrying than spending a few million pounds on a land deal. It was an area I had no experience of, knowing that I had to quickly develop this alien skill, drive to the office, deliver the letter, walk to the shop, call Noel, buy the right game, return to the car then drive back to the yard. This may sound simplistic and an everyday task to many people who undertake such missions on a daily basis, often with not one, but two, three, or even four little Joshes, a whole fleet of them even. To me however, it was a new skill to be learnt, no training, or practise under supervision from an experienced adult was available. It was straight in there, in at the deep end, like being asked to complete a land deal without a degree or any training.

So what do I do now? I thought, while pulling out of the yard to head into town. Not only did I have no experience of little people, but I knew nothing of gaming. Playing games on a games thing was also out of my knowledge, way out. To me, computer games and games consoles were a thing I had never experienced, computers were just for work. As it turned out, I need not have concerned myself in the slightest. I had a leading authority on them sitting here; right behind me in the back of my own car. How lucky was that? I listened to the ins and outs of all the games and the machine itself, not to mention what to do, my knowledge was dramatically increasing at a rate of knots by the minute.

"How do you know my Granddad then? Do you bring him lots of cars to break up like the big man?"

I paused for a moment, not to consider my response to the question, but to wonder what was meant by 'a big man bringing lots of cars'. This description and situation lead me to think immediately of Mark Daniels. Then again, it could have been a tall man, or one considerably out of shape, rather than one of muscle and power.

"I have an old MG Midget, so come to your Granddad for parts and advice." I chose not to mention the scrap yard deal, I did not know if little Josh realised that his favourite playground was soon to disappear for good. I am sure the collection, and level of adventure would soon be extended over at Noel's house. Then again, what was in the letter? Contracts were exchanged, so one way or another, the yard was going to go. Entertaining Josh was something that I had not needed to have worried about. In fact, it was more a case of me being entertained, while increasing my education. All I needed to do was to say a few words, after which a great deal of words were emitted as a response. In fact, some combinations of words were in effect questions, but ones where no replies were required as there was simply no pause in which to respond. We soon met the crawling stop-start traffic, paused at the traffic lights and turned into the edge of the business park where the office was located.

The office stood in a slightly elevated position, looking down across the crowded car park that from a distance resembled a multi-coloured field of corn. The busy main road with the edge of the retail sector lay across the road. The first shop that lay directly opposite the traffic lights was the games store, so much desired by little Josh. I had never entered the store, or even paused to look into the window as it was simply not my thing. I had noticed from the office window that at

Christmas and at other times through the year, crowds of people of all ages flocked to the store. The Christmas attraction was clear to me, people armed with long present lists. I had now just learnt all about how popular the release of a new game was, which had evaporated my theory, that they must be giving the merchandise away.

I turned left into the office car park, pausing at the barrier arm, which lifted as I held my security card out of the window. The movement seemed quicker today, usually the slow raising of the arm and having to pause the car, appeared to take an age when keen to gain entry to the building, to reach my desk, to switch on the computer, to clutch a pile of papers and to start to work with not a moment to lose. For some reason, every second of every moment had mattered, to be as productive as possible in a day. Now, that was all gone. I then started to hunt, stalking through the mass of cars, searching for a vacated space. Cars were double parked as usual and there was no obvious space, until I reached the office building. There was one free space under the building itself, the under-croft reserved for the directors and visitors. I pulled into the space next to the door, the space was being reserved for a visitor during the day, but currently free and after all, I was not going to be long. It also felt safer, having to leave Josh in the car while I acted as carrier pigeon.

"Stay there, Josh, I will be right back in a few moments," I said, leaving the radio playing to give him some entertainment.

I entered the rear door of the office and ran up the secondary staircase, mainly used as the fire escape, but also used as a quick route to the car park for the staff. The open plan area in which I worked was not populated, the team must be in a meeting, the chairs were deserted with files and plans of The Hub spread out on most desks. I could see through the glass partition that Scott's desk was also empty, his desk bare, totally uncluttered, maybe the sign of having nothing to do. In property there are always massive amounts of paperwork around, the nature of the job has items pending, waiting for progress, to be picked up when a phone rings, an email appears, or when data that is awaited arrives. Plans need space to be spread out for correct studying. He had obviously settled in quickly, various personal belongings furnishing the office, giving it a personal touch, right down to photographs of his travels placed around the walls.

Dean was out, too, his office more cluttered, with piles of files on the floor. I placed the envelope on his desk amongst the used coffee cups, either waiting for his Personal Assistant to collect, or to become a scientific experiment, prior to analysis. I made my exit, pausing for thought as to the whereabouts of the team, who I assumed to be in the board room. The timing was perfect. A quick entrance and exit without having to make polite conversation, whilst leaving evidence that I was working and had been in the office for an unidentified length of time. If this was a team meeting in the usual way, the duration could be of significant length, so as far as anyone realised, I may have been in for a while to attend to some urgent detail on the deal. As long as The Hub was to be delivered, that was all that mattered to Dean at this stage. Other matters, or any approach that did not reflect the image of his latest arrangement could wait until the scheme was on site. There was one question that remained unanswered, that was the obvious question; what was contained within the envelope?

I rushed back to the car using the same route as before, opened the door for Josh who bounced out of the car, unable to contain his excitement.

"I'll race you to the store, last one there is..." his words fading into the distance. He was off, at speed, great speed. Quicker than I ever imagined little legs could travel. Josh was heading across the sea of parked cars in the direction of the shops before I had time to utter a word. Luckily all cars in the car park were indeed firmly parked at that moment in time. No doubt afraid to move, as car removal from a space was unlikely to be followed by car replacement in an available space. I ran after him, not to partake in the competition of the race, but concerned of the safety aspect of him heading towards the busy main road. Cars and busses were passing by, starting from and pausing at the traffic lights as the colour patterns repeated. Josh was a distance away, clearly fully focused, with full intent on one target; the store. There was no space for thought about anyone, or anything else.

"Josh wait! Wait for me. Josh! JOSH!"

My heart was beating faster, a combination of the sudden, unexpected, strenuous exercise and the thought of not returning to the yard with Josh. What if something happened to him when I am entrusted with him for less than an hour? Not to mention having to make a call to Noel to say that something had happened to his precious grandson. My suit and formal shoes were hardly suitable attire for running. I was gaining distance on him towards the bottom of the slope, something that I may not have done on a wet day with smooth leather soled shoes that struggled for grip. I caught up moments before the pedestrian crossing, just as it turned to green, holding up a double-decker bus. It was clear, so we continued to run across. I think he would have stopped; I liked to think that he would have stopped, but then who knows? He was safe, nothing happened and it was history, soon to be forgotten as we entered the shop doorway to look at the games.

"Come on, I know where they are. Over here let's see what they have."

I followed as per my order, pulling my mobile phone out of my pocket. I dialled the scrap yard, Noel picking up the call after only three rings. Within the time for the phone to connect, little Josh had pulled out two games. The result of extensive research which had already been undertaken, not only as to what games were available, but also the layout of the store imprinted within his brain. I thought this task could take time; finding the children's section; choosing a suitable purchase; making a decision between several options, where his favourite quickly resonated between the different offerings. There was none of that. Straight in, straight to the section of the store, and little hands placed directly upon the chosen items. The whole exercise was undertaken in one swift movement. With such planning and forethought, combined with smooth execution, he should be good in years to come when applied to an employment situation.

"We are in the shop, the ones Josh likes both look suitable, nothing out of his age range, so how much do you want to spend?"

"He's a good lad, tell him his Granddad will buy him both, I will give you any extra money when you are back."

I ended the call and continued to read the games. "Are these the right ones?"

"Yes, of course they are, silly Billy."

He glanced up at me, prising his eyes from the boxes for a few valuable seconds, clearly not believing that I questioned, plus my ignorance in such items.

We turned to face the front of the shop, away from the back wall where we had been analysing the stock. Out of the shop window, the business park was in full view, the car park to the fore, with the office clearly visible, elevated in the background. There was an un-obscured view of my car, parked in its prominent position. I wondered just how long I had got to continue to work there, under the watchful eye of Scott. How controlling would he be with his new found powers? How much involvement in The Hub would he have? As soon as I had got through this week, I was to make my approaches. At least when the deal became public, it would help my reputation in the employment marketplace, providing that Scott, or Dean did not take all the credit for the deal. We started to move towards the till, Josh still excited with his purchase. People passed by the window, a combination of shoppers, young and old as well as business people rushing to and fro from the neighbouring offices.

Across in the office the envelope still sat unopened on Dean's desk, everyone unaware of what was contained within. My colleagues remained gathered together in the Board

Room, its title describing the mood of the team, as Scott talked at great length about the new procedures that he was to impose. Dean was there to offer support, to paint the new united picture that they had suddenly become the artists of.

I jumped with the sound of a loud bang outside of the shop, Josh jumped too, despite the intensity of his interest in his selected purchases. It sounded loud, too loud for a vehicle collision. Simultaneous to the sound, I could not believe my eyes as the boot lid and rear doors of my car were ripped off, flying into the air, the back end of the car lifting and falling rapidly. This was instantly followed by the higher pitched sound of glass shattering and landing on the tarmac below. Flames shot up under the under-croft from what was left of my car. They were leading up to the first floor of the building. The car was burning, burning fast. Shocked bystanders were watching in disbelief, others had screamed and were running, making their exit for an area of safety, some dropping bags as they fled. People started running about outside, people were leaving the offices through the front door, running to the edge of the car park, clearly in a state of hysterical panic.

Chapter 6

The Incident

Within the Board Room, Scott was preaching to his new team about procedures.

"I am introducing a new spreadsheet log; it is to be used to record all potential new business activity. If we can all ensure that this is updated on a daily basis, we can assess our thoughts without any maverick new business ideas evolving."

Nigel Hopkinson sat up in his chair, his short stature may not have got him noticed, but his raft of comments always did. He was the joker of the team and not taking the new lecture at all seriously, looking at ways to cause distraction, to make the long session slightly more bearable and remove some of the Board Room boredom.

"Scott, shall we develop a master spreadsheet that lists all other spreadsheets, and then we can update it each time we make changes to any other spreadsheet? It would be the master spreadsheet, spreadsheet."

Several of the team found Nigel's comment humorous, appreciating what he was attempting to do to Scott and his new raft of procedures. Something through the window then caught Nigel's eye, offering yet further distraction. He was witnessing a sight that was so unexpected to the extreme of challenging his vision of reality; he adjusted his metal rimmed glasses in a double take.

A familiar, suited figure, was running at speed away from the office, down towards the bottom of the car park, heading for the town. He nudged Tia who sat between him and the window. She was a graduate member of the team whom Nigel had recruited. She just happened to share the same characteristics as the secretary he had selected a few months previous; female; pretty; dark brown eyes; dark hair and an attractive figure. Both girls selected proved to be great assets to the company. Nigel took delight in his new image with the male members of the team, enjoying the highest position on the podium when it came to recruitment. Tia looked out, instantly assumed something must be wrong, and then making her excuses to visit the ladies, she vacated the room. The true reason for her interruption was to make a mobile phone call to establish if everything was alright. Tia had a calm, inherently kind hearted, caring way with her and was very much a people person.

Boredom came to a dramatic, sudden and terrifying end, as did Scott's debut performance. The room violently shook with the sound of a deafening explosion. The vibration resonated through the structure as the glass in the windows shattered inwards on to Tia's chair. The smell of burning plastic infiltrated the room through the void left by the window. The atmosphere changed instantly from professionalism with a little jollity, to hysteria, panic and survival. The reaction of the team was split, some sat clutching their chair, glued to the spot, others screaming in the panic and jumping off their chairs to exit the building. No fire alarm was sounding, but flames were licking up the building across the window outside, the windows on the stairway having also been shattered by the impact.

People flooded from the building, shouting about an exploded car as the sound of distant sirens grew in intensity. The fire warden moved into emergency mode, starting to establish who was in the building and if they were all accounted for, standing out from the dark suits with the high visibility vest and clipboard. The assembled party were checked as all present and correct. They looked back at the building with shattered windows and what was left of a familiar company Audi, parked in the under croft visitors spaces, flames rising from the rear. The front clearly remained intact, revealing the identity of the vehicle and in many eyes, the culprit of the explosion. Two other cars were damaged, parked adjacent to it, one of its rear doors lay battered near to the fire assembly point, as if it was fallout from an aircraft.

The full complement of emergency services arrived, the fire being rapidly extinguished. The quantity of police cars doubled, tripled, quadrupled, indicating the level of their interest as the area was sealed.

Crowds of onlookers appeared in the streets around, many lining the street in front of the games store. The assistants in the store spoke of the happenings, I tried to hide my shock, in total disbelief, acting as someone with no involvement. We paid for the games and headed towards the door. I had every intention to head across the road to the incident, having increased concerned about the team, and my car. The Thought then entered my head, it was my car that had exploded, yes my car, the car that Josh and I were in ten minutes earlier. How were we to get back? Why has it exploded? What about my colleagues?

Josh was fascinated by the excitement; in fact the sights and sounds of the police cars and fire engines seemed to rank higher than his games. I was sure however that this would be short lived and simply in the moment.

My mobile rang, it was Tia: "Are you alright?"

"Never mind about me, how are you? How are the others?"

"Your car just blew up and damaged the office windows, nearly killed us all, but apart from that just a normal day. Everyone is fine, just a couple of people with a few scratches from the glass and more than a little shocked."

“Shocked? I know the feeling! My car has just blown up a few minutes after I got out with Noel Harrington’s Grandson.”

“You were so lucky. Anyway, are you now a babysitter?”

“Noel was not happy about Scott changing the deal, he asked me to take an envelope to Dean, it is on his desk, and while I was at it I did him a favour and took little Josh to the game store.”

“Hang on, hang on…I am listening to something…Nigel saw you running from the car park just before the explosion, he has told Scott and Dean. They think you have tried to blow us all up as you did not get the Director Job. They are going over to talk to the police. I’d make yourself scarce for a while; it is getting a bit heated here about you. I think they are convinced you were out to get them.”

“What? Josh ran from the car when I let him out, I ran to catch him.”

“I’ll call you later, from my personal phone to yours.”

At that point a voice loudly bellowed through the crowd: “A man ran from the car to that shop, he had a kid with him...Get him! Quick he is there!”

Two large men came running in our direction, not looking the type to be argued with, both in casual dress. The police pulled up in front of the shop in a Volvo rapid response car. Two Police Officers got out, pulling a gun from the inbuilt locker, the doors being left open.

My heart was pounding, we had two choices; stay, or go. My brain analysed the situation in a fraction of a second. There was no time for logical thought, risk analysis, or making any form of considered decision. Adrenalin was taking over. The instant decision was to go, so we fled.

Running into town, more police were heading to the scene. There was no doubt we would quickly be identified. It was school holidays so there were children with parents around the shops not realising what had happened, but inquisitively looking around to try to see what was occurring.

CCTV would soon spot us, but the immediate problem where the two large guys who were both on to us. If they were police, they were well disguised, rather than the usual plain clothes detectives who look like, well, plain clothes detectives really. The first was well built, in his mid-forties, with mid-length slick back dark hair, wearing cargo trousers and a brown top. The second tended to stay in the background, but was even larger, with a shaved head, diamond earring, wearing a white tee-shirt and jeans. Neither looked particularly agile, but neither looked particularly welcoming either if contact was to be made.

I could not comprehend that many of my colleagues had thought that I had tried to blow them up, then again, it is not every day that I am promised a Directorship which is given to someone else, missing from a meeting, park my car in the reserved spaces under the building, then run away through the car park shortly before my car explodes and catches fire. I suppose there is a logical conclusion to be gained somewhere in all of that. I could not think of a single incident that had ever occurred while I had worked there that was anything remotely similar to one of those events, let alone the combination of them all and in that order.

“Keep moving Josh, let’s go in here.”

“Hey this is fun isn’t it? Who are those big men that are coming with us?”

“Oh, I think they are just a bit late for something.” I replied, hoping that I was soon not going to become 'late'. We quickly entered a 1960’s office block across the road. It was a typical multi-storey concrete building. It housed the solicitors that we used at work, so my face was familiar to the concierge, who acknowledged us from behind his desk as friendly as ever, as we took the lift up the building. Although the majority of the time he was paid to acknowledge visitors, direct them around the building, and take hand delivered or couriered packages. He also acted as security, so I was sure that the two men following would be challenged. Not that a tall, thin man with grey hair, in his late sixties would be able to do much to prevent their entrance. He was, I thought, like most people taking on that type of job at his age, a retired Police Officer, so if the two large followers where plain clothes detectives, he may well know them anyway.

We arrived at the fifth floor. I knew parts of the building from various meetings over the years. I was once told how the toilets and service area interconnected to the other half of the building that was occupied by a different company. I headed Josh in the direction that I thought it was, passing the double doors to the fire escape stairs. Moments after passing by they started to open, I glanced around as the shape of the first of the large men opened them. We ran through a pair of double fire doors in the long corridor that were shut. He was gaining on us. I pushed through the doors, telling Josh to keep going. Turning around, I forced the door shut as hard as I could, exerting pressure on the self-closure. One door was bolted closed, as I pushed against the free door, I kicked a wedge that was conveniently left on the floor for deliveries, under the bottom. As I kicked it in to position, a force was pushing silently from the other side, trying to force entry. I knew by the build of the man in pursuit, he would soon exert enough pressure on the door to push the wedge along the old vinyl tiled floor, but this was buying us a few seconds of shelter. The solid panel doors prevented our direction of travel from being immediately apparent.

I opened a door on the right at the very bottom of the corridor and entered, feeling around for a light switch, hoping to reveal a means of escape. The fluorescent light flickered on and off before slowly illuminating the room. We had entered a small room used as a store with no natural light. At high level on the left hand side was a small, rectangular window, fitted with obscure frosted glass. It was backlit with artificial light, what was once external, had now become internal, as the building had evolved and been extended over the years. It was an opening casement, but had long since been secured and painted over. I decided it was worth a go, moving a storage cabinet to lie directly beneath the window, I kicked out. The frame was too well secured to move. I tried again, this time taking aim at the glass; it shattered, revealing our intended destination, a toilet cubical on the other side.

"Quick Josh, I am going to lower you through this window first, wait on the other side while I climb through."

I picked Josh up and lowered him through the gap, still clutching his purchase of games, his knuckles turning white with the intensity of his grip on the little bag. It was however keeping him happy. So far he was enjoying the adventure of the day, something that even at his age would not have been dreamt about. Although it was a pain, and may have inhibited progress, I let him keep them just to keep the peace. The last thing that I needed right now was a dispute with an eight year old, especially one that I had only met hours before. I pushed myself through feet first, tearing my suit on the edge of the broken window; the tight squeeze deformed the natural shape of my body as I wondered if my shoulders would pass through. I was part way, almost wedged like a Champaign cork and could hear rushed, heavy footsteps behind me, doors being pushed open, frantically attempting to locate us. I fell onto the floor below as I heard the store room door open behind me.

Leaving the cubicle I noticed how much better this part of the building was, more tastefully refurbished in recent years. A vase of flowers stood on the vanity unit containing the wash hand basins. I opened the door to leave the toilets, starting to panic at not just the pursuit but also the situation. It was just starting to occur to me what had happened and this was reality, not some form of nightmare.

With the pain I had experienced, I knew that the dimensions of the window were small enough to keep the pursuer behind. He was well built, far larger than I and I found it a struggle. I then also remembered the other man. He had not been seen to physically enter the building from my last glimpse of him, back in the reception. Was he ahead of us, there to cut us off at any moment? Who were they and what were they doing? The adrenalin was still pumping around my body, I felt on a high. I tried not to think about the future consequences; after all I was now on the run. I did not know how I had got there. I had done nothing, but was now on the run from the police and if that was not enough, I was also being chased by these other two men.

I pulled open the door from the toilets, trying to anticipate what may lie ahead. As the door swung open, it felt light to the hand, the full weight of the door and its closure was clearly not felt by my arm. I thought of the men, but it turned out I was wrong, it was a young lady, which was not at all surprising when the symbol on the outside of the door was revealed.

"Oh, do you usually use the ladies?" she asked with a smile on her face, not being fazed by the meeting.

"Only when I am a bit lost, after having climbed through a window, while being chased by two large men." After all, what was I to say? She may have known I was not supposed to be in the building for all I knew, not to mention in the ladies toilets, with a trail of glass behind. She would either take it seriously, or in jest until she had considered the glass on the floor and possibly witnessed a large man, wedged in a small opening.

"Come now, what have you done?"

"Nothing at all, they just think I have blown my car up."

"So you only use the Ladies in exceptional circumstances then. I am Sally Henderson; a solicitor, I specialise in criminal law. Wait there two minutes as I really must go."

"The man may be trying to get through the window it may not be safe, although I struggled."

"It is not me he is after is it? I'll shout if he is there."

She soon returned from the toilets. What she had done I did not know, had she called the police? Were the men around and connected to her? I did not know why I had waited and had trusted her, but for some reason I had. There was no one else to trust and I needed assistance.

"How about you come with me, the back way to my offices and we will talk. It is your lucky day."

"Well I am a bit short of options at the moment and if this is a lucky day, well I..." I did not conclude the sentence, we both smiled and laughed. After the recent events, any coincidence did not strike me as in the least bit strange.

We moved off, heading down the service lift to the car park, chatting instantly like long lost friends, filling Sally in on the details. She was middle to late twenties, around my age, slim, but not too thin having the right curves, small build, short to medium height, dark brown hair with red highlights, her white teeth contrasting with her tanned skin and large, sparkling dark brown eyes. Probably the prettiest person I had ever seen. Clearly, in this situation she was also the female version of the knight in shining armour. We ran up from the end of the ramp of the car park at the edge of a shopping centre. Running after her, even in the circumstances, I now felt quite relaxed and could not help but notice she was as aesthetically pleasing from the rear as from the front.

Police were everywhere, they were also no doubt spying on every slight movement that everyone made through CCTV, so there was little chance to transverse the town unnoticed. We were in the pedestrianised area, as we ran towards the shopping centre then turned into an elegant, white stone building that had previously been a bank prior to conversion into offices.

There was no sign of the two large men. We were watched by the rider of one of two police horses; one grey and one bay. Whether it was their elevated vantage point on the beautiful mount, or a radio call tip-off from CCTV monitoring I did not know, I thought as we entered the building that we had been spotted.

We headed for the basement of the clean, tidy offices that had clearly been interior designed. As we entered the room I looked at the door, it was around 300mm thick. Sally bolted it shut from the inside with the integral mechanisms that secured the room. I was not now being physically chased, but was locked in a former strong room, discussing the events of the day and the background as to how I had arrived there. Then again, if I had got to be locked in a room with someone, then Sally would probably be at the most prominent position of the list. Josh was now getting fed up and starting to show it. It had been a long day and he understood only parts of what was happening. It was arranged for him to go back to Noel; the police could interview him there in familiar surroundings, as soon as this discussion had reached its natural conclusion.

"We have not got long, the police are here. They will arrest you. Something that exploded is a big deal to them. I will put them right on a few things, as I have a few connections and then represent you. Say nothing about the happenings unless I am present. Talk about anything, but not the property deal, directorship, Noel Harrington, large men, or any of today's explosive events. Now let's run through the detail of today once more."

I reiterated the happenings again, in detail, exactly where I had been, what I had said, what everyone else had said, piece by piece reliving every moment of the day. It had certainly been an experience that I would never forget. I just did not realise at that moment just how key to the rest of my life, the events would turn out to be.

"The starter motor! The fucking starter motor. Fucking Harrington! He has done this, set me up to get revenge on the company for changing the deal. He put the starter motor in the boot of the car, for me to take home. He never showed it to me, just placed it in the boot and shut the lid when I went over to fetch Josh. The bastard! The cunning old bastard. That is where the police should focus."

"We do not mention this to the police. It is not the way we are going with this. No "B" word, there was no bomb. Got that? No matter what happens, we are not talking bombs here, they are terrorism. The Terrorism Act is not the answer. If anything goes wrong it would be worse, far worse."

"What about Noel Harrington? He has done this. He has got me in this position, nearly blew me up, my colleagues, then he may have got me locked up for the next ten years!"

I was starting to lose my cool. I had been through a lot today. The stress was starting to show through, the reality hitting home about the situation I was now facing.

"Look, just do not go there. That is not the direction we are going with this. Got that? I specialise in representing criminals, true criminals, or people that society, or the police, view as criminals that is. There is a huge difference there, when stories and outlooks on life are realised. There will be an innocent explanation in all of this. Just the usual police overreaction; if something makes a bang; people expect it to be a bomb. That is the public reaction, wanting subconsciously, or consciously, to be in on the action, the big news story, how they survived and witnessed it. They can tell their children in years to come. Get interviewed by the press, appear on television, getting labelled a hero, all for doing nothing, just happening to be there. The police go along with what the public want them to do. They will react, or more importantly be seen to react. It is a precaution, why would they think deep down that there was a bomb here with no political target and it was not just an accidental explosion?"

"Well you have clearly been here before, so I will go along with you. I will say what you have told me to say. Remember if it goes wrong though, I need you to get me out and suddenly find the truth."

The story, and part of it *was* a story, a simple act of fiction was rehearsed and ready to be revealed to the police. The door was opened, I knew what was going to happen, with me being picked up from the rear of the building in a not too friendly manner. The officer – I was sure – wanted to catch a bomber for his Curriculum Vitae; he was hoping for a small struggle that he could become the hero of. Unfortunately I was to disappoint with the struggle, and intended to further water his fire over arresting a bomber, too.

Chapter 7

Four Walls

I had always had faith in the police and elements of the criminal justice system. I had believed that if someone was questioned, this would not be carried out without good reason. If someone was being detained, then the police would almost certainly have got a guilty party. Whether they could prove it or not, well, that was a totally different matter. Along with this, I also believed the inverse, which went hand in hand with the first belief. That if you did not commit a crime, then you were not going to get accused of committing one. That you would never be treated as a criminal, if you were not one. A simple logical thought, until now that was.

After all, to be fair, they are only going on what has been said to them, what the results of investigations are. What people think they have observed and what CCTV has illustrated. This only covers the illusion of what has been, or appears to have been carried out on stage. Not what has actually happened, not what happened just out of view, behind the curtain, or what was not seen by the person sitting behind a pillar, a tall man, or a lady wearing a big hat? The missed events during the long play entitled; 'life'.

The record of events and sightings to someone with an obscured view may be the truth, the whole truth and nothing but the truth to them. It is however incomplete, inaccurate, misleading and misinterpreted, although maybe for all of the right reasons. Beauty may be in the eye of the beholder, but the truth is not. We all only ever observe and know what we experience. We as individuals experience a fraction of any story, as there is usually more than one person involved. In any event, no one knows for sure, or even at all, what someone is truly thinking, what their actual intentions, thoughts, or actions are. They are protected from the stage by the big curtain. That is only considering intended actions. There is then the unintentional blocking of the stage by the lady in the big hat.

To add further there is the individual human brain, the interpretation of what we see. How certain occurrences are sifted through and catalogued as important, or significant. What is considered of significance is a simple analysis and categorisation at the moment in question. The ranking is sure to change as time or experiences evolve, as we journey through the tunnel that life is, as the story becomes revealed.

A move to the right may seem the correct thing to do, and in fact, may well be the appropriate thing to do at any moment. In ten, fifteen, or twenty years' time, moving to the left may have yielded the greater benefit in the long-term, even if there was short-term disadvantage, or pain. Take the dentist; we visit them for short-term torture, or unpleasantness, with the aim of preventing long-term, more severe pain. The rest of life is not so clear. The filing system of the brain may therefore be inaccurate, or misleading, requiring constant attention by the secretary to ensure that files are in order for immediate audit. The results of alternative actions are never known, no analysis, modelling and testing can prove a result. Life is a null hypothesis.

Am I psychologically disturbed? Are we all psychologically disturbed? Is the accepted normality, actually abnormality? Is what the majority of people would view as insanity actually sanity?

Here I was in this mess, in the middle of the night, considering theories that have never approached the front of my brain. My colleagues, friends, the public, all thinking I had committed some offence. Meanwhile Noel Harrington played at home with Josh, learning how to play the two new games. I was sure they would be full of action too, almost as much as the day's events.

The police appeared to be in no hurry. They were either holding me here while they compiled evidence as they needed more, or to establish details from all the willing witnesses. They, no doubt all wanted to play their part in the story, some dangerously wanting to become authors and directors, in addition to their role as extras. Alternatively, was it an interrogation, sorry, negotiation technique to see if I would lose my cool and confess to all? Maybe someone from the other end of the country would hear about all of this on the news, make a full confession, even if they were sitting at home alone at the time, demonstrating their culinary skills in the preparation of beans on toast. It happens on television, so someone must have got it from somewhere. They may confess to all, and then get found guilty. After all, I may get found guilty and I have carried out no more of a criminal act today than they have.

The cell was depressing, I had never seen one before and I paced up and down, being too restless to sit. I was walking around the small cell, making sure I had all details clearly in my head of the story that Sally had decided would be the truth. In fact, the more I rehearsed it in my head, the more it became the truth, the whole truth, and nothing but the truth. I was now convinced that the account of what had happened was how it actually was. The thoughts of what I believed to have happened were still there, lingering in the background of my mind, filed to the rear of my brain, in a bring-forward filing system to be forgotten for the moment, but brought forward in the future.

I could not believe how noisy it was, the empty rooms echoed. A couple of people had been detained that were particularly vocal, a combination of frustration, aggression and alcohol mixed together in a volatile cocktail. Combined with this, they did not sound the most educated of individuals to start with and certainly were not demonstrating much English reserve.

I paced around my cage again, like the captive zoo animal that I had become. Deprived from my natural habitat and frustrated by captivity, being retained for doing a legal favour for someone. I was removed from my habitat, the mammals who I knew, my home, my surroundings and natural sources of food. The behaviours were now imposed, thrust upon me by removal from the wild and the way that I lived. I wanted to walk fast, or run, to undertake exertion, but there was no place to go, so instead paced another lap of the cell, levels of frustration increasing without outlet.

The door opened. I was led firmly to an interview room, the story telling was about to commence.

Sally was present, looking just as attractive, but with her hair tightly stretched and tied up. The soft, friendliness replaced by a severe, serious side, clearly meaning business.

The two plain clothes officers sat before me. One tall, thin, around thirty-five years of age, fresh faced with short ginger hair. He was introduced as Detective Inspector Ryan. The second officer was shorter, older, maybe around fifty-five, with thinning brown hair, and a well weathered red face. He was less senior despite his age, being a Detective Sergeant Armstrong. He looked as if he would be more at home on a farm, out in the fresh air, or with a bottle of whiskey than sitting in a Police Station. I suspected he was someone who enjoyed the role out in the field, chatting with the informants, chasing the animals of society, rather than sitting in the station, completing endless paperwork. I believed this to be a game of contrast between the two of them. Armstrong had a more relaxed approach than Ryan. He was obviously intending to play the 'good cop' role of the duo. Ryan was the opposite, he was clearly destined for the top, or at least, he thought that he was. His whole attitude suggested that nothing, and no one was to get in his way. His interest was the rule book, the procedures, the reports to be filed, the statistics to be met and not out there mixing with the animals. He clearly believed his place was behind the desk, ordering the likes of Armstrong around, the foot soldiers that carry out the traditional policing and like his colleague, only get a whiff of promotion through the length of time served.

Everyone was sitting comfortably, well, the other three were as the formalities commenced. I went through the story for a second time. Picking Josh up and the letter; Noel looking in the boot of the car as the central locking had developed a fault, with the electric release only working sporadically and randomly; dropping the letter off at the office; Josh running off towards the shops with me following to catch him before he reached the road and caused an accident; Noel calling to ask if I can pick a game up for Josh; heading into town and wondering what was going off; hearing that something had happened to my car when I received a phone call from Tia while on the way to my solicitors office for advice on changes to the Construction Act. I was then picked up and detained for doing absolutely nothing. I concluded that I was as shocked and confused about the events as anyone else.

Armstrong rocked back on his chair; Ryan sat forward leaning across the table in a slightly intimidating manner.

"What was in the boot of your car sir? I mean everything, every little item. Every single spec of dirt."

"The spare wheel, tools that came with the car, my high visibility site coat, high visibility vest, hard hat, rigger boots, an old starter motor off my classic car, a can of petrol and some fertilizer."

I had managed to recall all the items that we had discussed earlier in the day, and awaited my game show winnings.

"Tell me about the starter motor, petrol and fertilizer then."

"Well simple, my starter motor was not working on my old MG, so I took it off to see if I could get it repaired at some point. I was going to drop in at a car electrical specialist when

I was out and about. The petrol can was for the lawn mower, the fertilizer was from my dad for the lawn after I mowed it."

"Do you usually carry such items? Were they secured?"

"I have just said about the starter, the gardening stuff, only when I need it; at this time of the year. The petrol can was a proper one that I have had for years. They were all just placed in the boot. I was to do the garden tonight, or was it last night?"

"Where and when did you get the petrol and fertilizer, petrol is not gardening stuff."

I reiterated the story, being vague about the source. Sally interjected.

"May I remind you DI Ryan that there is no law about carrying petrol in a correct safety can for a lawn mower. As for trying to get your lawn to grow, it is summer, when lawns grow and need cutting."

Ryan changed direction.

"Why were you parked under the building? We have witnesses saying they saw you run away from the car."

"It was the only place to park and Josh was in the car, so I wanted it close to the office door. Like I said, I ran to catch Josh when I let him out of the car."

"The witness says you were running alone, no kid."

"I was not with him, he was ahead of me, and he had run to the town to buy something."

"What about the central locking then? Why did someone that you had a business relationship with concerning property look at it? The car is under warranty, company car, too, so at no cost to you."

"I just mentioned it in passing that there was a fault, that is why I placed the letter that he gave me on the passenger seat and not in the boot, in case it was stuck there until I could get the boot fixed. The petrol and fertilizer had been there a few days as I had not been able to get them out. Mr

Harrington thought it may be trapped not an electrical fault, but he was wrong."

I answered the questions repeatedly, giving the same responses to the slightly amended phrases that I was being battered with. I was becoming frustrated, desperately wondering why they did not seem to believe me. While I was sounding like a stuck record. The story had slight modifications but that was down to Sally, not down to me. At the end of the day, I had done nothing wrong.

Ryan sat bolt upright, becoming agitated and raising his voice.

"Let us get one thing straight, we have witnesses. You were not given the job of Director that you were promised. A day or so later you parked your company car directly under the building, near the side door where you never park and should not park. You just happened to have the explosive combination of an electrical fault, petrol and fertilizer in the boot. You then ran, at speed, away from your car towards town. The car then just happened to explode moments later. A diesel car, diesel does not just explode. You did not return, but ended up in town at your solicitors. That is not good, not looking good at all. Maybe you would like to go away and think a little further about it, just to recollect that you have not got anything confused, or forgotten anything?"

DI Ryan was starting to get louder, his words starting to change from a rant into a slow shout, like the stereotypical Englishman abroad, thinking that someone speaking another native language will understand, loud and slow. The interview was over, well, at least for the time being and I was returned to my cage, cooped up once more. Sally was chatting to DS Armstrong as I was marched off.

Then adrenalin was running out, I was losing energy, being sapped dry through a combination of frustration and the day's events. Not being able to comprehend why they would not believe me. I thought hard about the truth. Why Sally had chosen the direction that she had. Was it to protect me? Was it to protect Noel? Who was she really representing here? Someone's best interests were being considered and the other party's interests were a mere consequence. Did she really appear at the ladies toilet by coincidence? Who were the two large men, and where did they go? I had a head bursting at the seams with questions, but not many answers. Any answers that I could conclude only guided the way to further, unanswered thoughts. Time passed, it must have been morning, the noise from the alcohol-fuelled guests had ceased. I was tired and sat down.

The door opened, I must have dozed off for a while. I was confused as to where I was and what was happening. I soon recalled the harsh, barely believable, reality of the events and what I was now being accused of. The fog of my mind was lifting, revealing the bright, blinding light that may well continue to hurt my eyes.

Chapter 8

The Difference a Day Makes

I was led down the corridor to the area of the Police Station where I was first taken on my arrival. My belongings were returned to me, I was free to go. In the entrance, a now familiar figure stood there. Her hair was now down and flowing, glinting in the daylight, the softness having returned. She was now my chauffeur home as we walked to her black Porsche Boxster.

"Why?" I asked as I sat in the firm black leather seats. The single word was all that my brain could manage to say.

"Why not? It is the truth. The justice system works. It was a simple over reaction to an accident. An electrical fault combined with the explosive concoction of your car boot. The police have investigated fairly, detained the suspect, established your innocence and released you."

"But aren't you forgetting something? The truth! Harrington, the fact that the car is diesel, there was no petrol can in the car and no fertilizer for the lawn. I have also travelled 50,000 miles in that car in its two years and it has never developed any fault."

"The police investigated and realised it was an accident, the scene of crime officers found that you had petrol and fertilizer in the boot. The electrical fault from the central locking and boot release was enough to cause the accident. It is therefore the truth. It is fact. That is what happened."

I decided not to question further, I realised it was wrong, all wrong, but that I was free, which was right. I knew that this had been a set up and was sure it was Noel, maybe with a little assistance from Mark Daniels.

Anyway, I was free, clear of offenses and slightly amused by the situation.

"I gave Scott and Dean a scare though. I got my own back on the office without even trying. I am just not sure they will want me back though, not after all this. They may still blame me for the event." There were no messages left on my mobile, not even from Tia, as we reached my home.

"Why would you want to return? After all, look how they have treated you."

I understood the point; it was rational, logical thinking. There was the basic need of employment, the requirement for money to pay the mortgage, maintain the car, to cloth and feed myself. The fundamental requirements of modern 'developed' man were still there, they had not been dropped, and evidence still strongly supported their need, without any doubt.

"You must know what the property market is like. Where would I go to work? People will soon know the deal I pulled off, even if Scott and Dean try to take the credit I can try to correct that. But surely, that is a little insignificant, compared to the person who blew his company car up along with part of the office when he did not get promotion. I know which I would find the most memorable. Just think of the inevitable question on an application form, or at interview: So why did you choose to leave your last job? Oh, I accidently blew my company car and the bloody office up!"

I started to laugh. We both started to laugh, seeing the funny side of the events and the situation. Sally replied, posing as an interviewer.

"Well, as the office has been repaired and no major damage was done, it was obviously most poorly executed indeed. Would you like to say what you would do differently in the future, as the project clearly failed?"

We entered the house, went straight to the kitchen and reached for a bottle of vodka to celebrate. I did not look at the time, I was not bothered. I was out, free, and it had been proved an accident. We opened another bottle and merrily drank the content. I knew that I would make contact with Noel if he did not contact me, but for now, that could wait. I was having fun. More fun than I had ever endured before. The future concerning what I would do, how I would pay the mortgage, and indeed survive, could just wait. It was about now, about the moment.

We looked straight into each other's eyes, holding the moment for a while, the dark brown sparkly gems deep and expressive, we turned to embrace, kissing gently.

"Shall we celebrate? I think I deserve a big thank you for getting you off don't you? Now it's my turn to get off."

Sally turned, pushing me back on the sofa and lay above me. We touched each other for the first time, something that despite the situation, I feel we had both wanted to do from the first, strange moments of meeting. My mobile rang; I left it, not noticing anything apart from the intensity of the situation and the beauty that was slowly, gently, calmly and lovingly, becoming connected to me.

We chatted, ate, drank then eventually retired to the bedroom. The velocity of the proceedings gained momentum. Although we had connected in a tender way downstairs, the intensity and passion now increased. We quickly removed each other's clothes, with a passion and high level of energy. It turned out a wild, passionate night, not being able to get close enough to each other. The following day brought a lie in for us both, the unanswered mobile starting to ring more and more frequently. Everything felt right, I knew that this was how things should be in the future and that we should make it last. It may be a strange situation, but so what.

Eventually I decided that the phone must be answered, that the reality needed to be addressed in able to sustain the fantasy, which had, itself, become a reality. Without the business addressed, the passion could not continue alone, it may be fuel for life, a driving force, but cannot alone sustain survival.

It was Tia, I took the call.

"Are you alright? I was worried."

"I am fine, had a day or so in a police hotel, though, until they realised it was an accident. What is the news?"

"We have been told it was all an accident, but Scott, Dean and Nigel are still questioning it. We are all working from the new office development that we completed last week while our office is being repaired. It was quite exciting really."

"What was the letter from Noel?"

"It was some plans, historic ones, with a letter claiming that the site will have archaeological interest, photographs showing some Roman artefacts that he said he dug up when excavating it for something. He had always kept it quiet but had copied the letter to the Planners. He is obviously proceeding with the deal, but trying to get his own back by causing a delay."

I ended the call, wondering if Noel was innocent in all of this and I had got everything wrong. Somehow deep down however, I thought not. I returned to carry on the celebration where we left off.

From that first day onwards we spent all of our time together, either at my house, or staying at Sally's executive apartment if we were heading towards town. It was the typical executive two bedroom penthouse, of contemporary design, electronic gimmicks and balcony overlooking the town. Sally said little about work; after all, she was not a property conveyancing, or family lawyer. She defended the underworld and was closely involved with them. Not just locally, but regionally, and sometimes further afield.

Sally was often called out in the middle of the night to support her clients after some dawn raid, or arrest. That was all part of Sally and after all, this is what had brought us together. To me, I had been introduced to the environment as an alien, by a turn of events that I had not controlled, a new environment that I had stumbled across when I tripped and fell into this new world. It was a total accident, without any control of my landing. My only conscious action that I had made was to reach out with my arms to break my fall, resulting in only grazing to the hands. I was enjoying the new world; it had injected happiness and life into my existence, redefining enjoyment, recalibrating what I had previously classified as happiness.

I accepted the new environment as the normal, and was becoming relaxed with my new habitat. It took little adjusting to, as I was led by Sally, I just chose not to think too much about some of the detail or the direction, and did not question the reasoning. The people I met were great, who some of them really were, what some of them did, their role and involvement I did not know, or want to know, but they were fine with me. For Sally it was different, this was her chosen environment, one that made her money, one that she was clearly totally at home and comfortable with. Besides she was a lawyer, on the right side of legality, providing a legitimate service for those who needed to execute the right for a defence. For Sally, this all seemed to be her natural habitat. That said, most of the time we kept ourselves to ourselves, spending time together without external intrusion. That is what we liked. To be together, just the two of us, that was all that mattered.

We were close, as close as it gets, there was only one missing item; her family. This was the one taboo subject, the one thing that was not discussed. She had one sister, her mother having tragically died from cancer when she was only a young child.

Her father was still around, although he was the one person whom she would not converse about. They were obviously still close, identified by the way that she reacted to him on the telephone, but he was someone whom I had never met. Whenever a call was taken, it tended to be accompanied by relocating to a different room. She would visit him, but the look of her soft, expressive eyes turned harder, like the compact dark earth of a sun-baked ploughed field if I probed too far. There was something missing, something that I was not being told, but I knew that and accepted that. Maybe it was me that he would just not approve of, something about my career, or how we met despite my innocence? Alternatively did Sally's line of work put strain on the relationship, he could be a Police Chief Constable or something for all I knew.

Two people could still be as close as we were to each other, but hide items, or events from one another. Why not? Everyone is an individual, with their own personality, thoughts, brain and character. We had full trust in each other and loved each other dearly. That was all that mattered. Sally would talk about him, or introduce us when she was ready, if she was ready. I was sure that I would know the detail one day, in her time she would reveal all and I would comprehend why she had made the decision that she had. I respected that, it was part of her and the respect that I had for her as a person.

What I did witness was the respect that the underworld and security industry gave her. She clearly worked for them on a regular basis and it paid well. Money was not an object. Every time we visited a club, Sally would be on a pedestal, we were always given the red carpet treatment. Then again, it was no surprise with her style, personality and aesthetically pleasing looks, accentuated by some little black number. We were treated as celebrities by the security staff and bar owners, no waiting in line like sheep for the sheep dip, or being herded together by door staff for us. We jumped the patiently waiting line of customers, walked straight in, never paying. We also rarely paid for drinks. I assumed that most of the door staff and club owners had history, something to hide, that Sally had worked her magic for them, just as she did for me. If that was not the case, they knew whom she was and were aware that they may well need her services in the near future. Free drinks flowed, usually followed by a hot night in the apartment.

Although Sally was a Solicitor, and I was a Surveyor, we did not completely fit in well with the professions. I was happy playing with my classic cars, Sally her modern, high powered cars, both having a gentle love of the country. The pretentious Law Society Dinner and Royal Institution of Chartered Surveyors Ball were not venues for us. We did not really mix with the colleagues of the same professional background, not being part of the 'in crowd' on the local scene. Both professions had their own meeting grounds at bars in town, where the packs would gather to make fun of any practice that chose not to participate. The country pub complete with a bar meal, was more a venue for us. Not that we always opted for the quiet life, a few drinks and dance at a local club was also welcomed when we were in the right mood. Well I say dance, for Sally that was indeed true, she could move, really move, and if walking through the crowds from the bar to the dance floor, she would stand out, be an exhibition amongst the crowds. As for me, well, I was hopeless, but then again, did it really matter how poor I looked? The 'dad dancing' from a youngster may not have appeared right, but I had a great time and how could I not, when with Sally?

Her gorgeous physical appearance, her voice, her opinions and her personality, plus a small quantity of mystery, all individually forming the perfect ingredients of a cocktail, which for me at least, had an effect vastly superior to that of alcohol, or any illegal substance.

I did pause for thought occasionally about her role and what her clients did for a living. If a shooting occurred; if it was gang, or drug related, or if a crime made the news, I knew Sally would be busy defending, working late at night, presumably to ensure that everything legal was in place. There was also the service of legal advice, to prevent events escalating to risky heights if any dispute was starting. I began to understand that people's whole lives depended upon the Jury, the thoughts of a few random, ordinary people, that were gathered together, against their free will, with the beliefs, stereotypical views, programmed brains regarding normality, and what they believed to be right.

As for my career, I was doing well. Part of the time I was giving property advice, mainly for clients of Sally, or people introduced to me by Mark Daniels. Most of the time they were interested in property development, or investing in small parcels of land close to potential future development land. They had the intention to speculate, take risks for the outcome of making large returns on small, key, ransom strips. The property market was in decline, interest rates on savings were low, this led to those lucky enough to have some surplus cash around being able to purchase land, or property, at discounted prices. Even larger developers were looking at the disposal of land to increase their liquidity, or discounting development properties, particularly in the residential market, leading to increased turnover. At the end of the day, these could be rented out in the short-term, and would, without doubt, increase in value and offer good returns, if an investor could afford to tie their money up for a few years. Fewer properties were also being built as a result of the declining property market, again, an ingredient for future returns when demand increases.

They were also interested in business opportunities, often small scale businesses that survived by cash payments. How many people pay the window cleaner, the hand car wash, or the burger van by anything other than cash? This was the type of business where the success of sales and the extent of the customer base, could not be easily identified. Cash generators, which relied on staff paid by cash.

They also had the added advantage of making cash legitimate, made it an open, honest living, allowing tax to be paid. This being the exact opposite of what most of the population aim to do, but following action to prevent money laundering, estate agents and garages had stopped taking tens of thousands of pounds in crumpled, used notes. Buying an exotic car, or house with several plastic carrier bags, or briefcases stuffed with the afore-mentioned rectangular pieces of paper, with Queen Elizabeth's face printed on one side, and a famous inventor or explorer on the other, was no longer an option. Not that I would have turned them away, if someone approached me with such a cargo, it would have been viewed an attractive proposition. I was sure that I would always be able to find a use for it.

When I was not involved in property, I tidied up classic cars and sold them, only concentrating on high quality vehicles that were sound, but needing benefit from cosmetic action. I mainly specialised in good examples of MG's, but also other affordable classics. The exotic cars with their advanced, expensive, or highly stressed components, were not for me. I lived near to a classic car dealer, who specialised in expensive, top quality offerings that people would travel miles to view, often rare models attracted customers from other countries. I was able to sell my top quality, but everyday classics through them on a commission basis, using their reputation, and they knew that any car I supplied would be to my high standards. It worked well, I always had my old friend Noel Harrington to assist me and supply parts. He taught me a great deal, and supplied parts from his scaled down business, run from the re-roofed outbuildings at his house. There was no great return in this as the vehicles I improved were relatively low value, but for me, working from my own garage, I had no real overhead to cover.

There was one item that I did not discuss with Noel, which was the small subject of explosions. I knew he was behind it, he knew that I knew it too, but we remained silent on the matter. I was angry deep within, but he ensured that Josh and I were safe before any explosion was triggered, and ultimately he had done me a favour. Firstly, he got me away from my employer who clearly did not value my input. Then there was the main result of the explosion; Sally. Without the events, we would not be together, I would not have found the love of my life and he knew it. To be fair, I enjoyed the new lifestyle that I had been given, and I was making a mint, far more than a directorship would have done. I also enjoyed the quality of life, to be able to do what I wanted, when I wanted, and spend time doing what I loved. My work was strictly legal, it was giving advice and that was all. How the money had originated, or any underlying reason for a property transaction, was simply none of my business. Sally was the same, a lawyer so on the right side of the law.

There was however, one slightly questionable line of work that I had become involved in for Mark. I was not sure what it was about, or wanted to know what it was about. I liked to think that it was legal, but deep down I was not sure, or at least, decided that I was unsure, as a position of self-reassurance. If I considered it in depth, delving below the most superficial, shallow, calm surface, the legality would be seriously in question. That was of course the classic car runs. The mutual enjoyment of driving a classic car, with other enthusiasts as a pack, was on the face of it, a totally innocent pastime.

The question was; what was I simultaneously moving around the country, or between countries along with the car? What suspicious package was added to the car when unattended? If of course anything at all, it may also have been a simple way of creating enjoyment for someone, when a courier was needed. Anyway, Mark paid for me to carry out this activity. I enjoyed myself with others on such events. I did not actually know that there was anything illegal, incorrect, or immoral involved. As far as I was concerned it was legal. I had never identified any suspicious item within the car, but then again, I had never looked for one. That was the way it was to stay. Sally knew about it and was happy with the situation. My naive approach was that if anything went wrong, I had legal support of my innocence, plus a character reference from other enthusiasts I regularly met on the trips.

I crawled from under Noel's traction engine to answer my phone, he was getting older, and the contortions often needed when restoring a vehicle were now beyond him, an ability that had fled, never to be returned. I enjoyed working with him and lending a hand when I could. It was Sally, she was excited about something. It was clear from her bubbly, quick voice that she was trying to contain something.

"I have some really exciting news, can't wait to see you. Meet me at Rendezvous at six. I have a meeting there until then."

"Six! I have to wait another two hours to see you? How will I manage?"

"I'm worth it. I'm always worth waiting for. You know that." Sally said changing the excitement to a slow, sexy voice.

I turned up at the bar five minutes earlier than arranged; the person Sally had been meeting was just turning to leave. They shook hands; a large, stocky figure, with slicked back dark hair, wearing a long black mohair coat, clearly looking like a member of the bars door staff. He turned to head towards the door, as he did so; I caught a passing glimpse of his face. He also caught sight of me, and I am sure that he realised that I had recognised him in an instant. It was months since I had last seen him, in the corridor of a 1960's office block, in hot pursuit of someone; me.

"Hi darling, I have been longing to speak to you tonight just wanting the meeting to end." Sally's excitement in her voice, eyes and smile was clearly exhibited for all to view.

"The man you met. Who is he?"

"Just a client, he works for Ma—" I interrupted, not waiting for the sentence to be completed.

"Mark? He works for Mark. He was the guy chasing me around after my little incident. I have no doubt."

"That is all over long ago, history. Yes, you are right. The two large guys that chased you work for Mark, they were not police, and they were ensuring you fled, making sure you headed in a direction away from the office so that stories made sense. They were to reach you before the police, not to get, or harm you in any way."

I smiled; this just confirmed what I had always suspected. I was not angry; I was pleased. The whole set up after all, had brought me to Sally, and that was real.

"What is the news then, you sounded fit to burst on the phone?"

"I am, well, I will be, in about eight months' time."

We grabbed hold of each other and kissed, the news was fantastic, I had enjoyed spending time with little Josh when he was at Noels and now we were to have our own package of joy.

"You can't take it back and change it like you do with your clothes and cars, Sal."

"I just hope it comes with instructions, I know nothing about them. My sister is only two years younger than I, so I was too close in age to realise anything."

We disposed of my house and Sally's penthouse, combining some of our savings. Our bank balances had also been reproducing at an amazing rate, not to mention the rectangular pieces of paper with the Queens head on, that I often came across. The Victorian gothic masterpiece of brick artwork became ours.

Alice was born. She was a beautiful little parcel, clearly taking after her mother. We now resided in Utopia.

Chapter 9

Leaving Utopia

We got Alice to sleep; at ten years of age looking after an offspring should become easier. Going to bed, getting dressed, and deciding what she wants, should all be routine actions, undertaken without the need for parental support. It should therefore be possible to restore some of the aspects of life that have to be sacrificed, when a young child is totally dependent upon its parents for survival. With an autistic child with severe learning delays, this is not at all the case; the level of dependence is, in fact, greater. A fast moving little person, having no understanding of danger and lacking the skills to master the routine aspects of life, is, believe me, harder. It therefore became increasingly difficult as time progressed.

At least with a baby, it is possible to take them out to dinner, sit them at the side of you while they sleep through the evenings proceedings. This is exactly what we did for the first year or so, where a contented little person sleeps, or looks around throughout a meal in a country pub. This is not the case with a finger feeding ten year old, who may well hurtle food across the room at other diners if it is not quite what she would like. That almost sounds like poor behaviour to the uninformed, but of course, that is far from the case. Poor behaviour can be controlled and corrected as there is the level of understanding, which is needed to reason and bargain with the youngster.

Alice's determination grew stronger, but not accompanied by the ability to talk and express what she wanted, it added to her frustration. This caused her to self-harm more frequently. Right from being born she was the loudest around, outperforming the other new-borns within minutes of birth, but this had not been developed into speech over time. If it had, maybe we would struggle to ever get a word in edgeways, but instead we had to rely on pointing as communication. This combined with her hyperactivity and difficulties sleeping, led to our difficulties sleeping, not that we had insomnia, just a lively ten year old at any time of the day, or night. Initially her development was very good, but deteriorated within hours of her combined triple vaccination for; Measles, Mumps and Rubella, resulting in being taken to hospital with a high temperature and suddenly deliberately banging her head on the floor.

Peace and quiet now filtered through the house. The only question being how long this would last. It was seven-thirty, as we lay upon the sofa for a while, listening out as if on guard to establish if the peace was to remain. We retired to the hot tub, naked, kissing and touching each other below the bubbles. We then relocated to bed, fuelled with the same passion as the celebration on that day when it all began. The surroundings were a little grander, with stone arched windows on two elevations; a grand carved four poster was the centrepiece of the room. None of that mattered however; the entertainment that we could produce ourselves, was all that was needed, without requiring any of the frills that money had created.

Sally's mobile rang, it was work. The mood changed, by the tone of her voice it was clearly a major occurrence and her services were needed. Unlike the usual calls, on this occasion she sounded genuinely concerned, on the verge of being upset about the news. The element of compassion usually expressed, was accompanied with a business-like authority and professionalism. On this occasion that element was lacking.

"God, no, I'm so sorry, the one night we get Ali to sleep on time and I have to go out. I may be a while; it sounds as if it could take some sorting."

"Is everything OK?"

"Yes, just work, but I am related to this one – my Little Sis is in trouble."

"I'll be waiting for you, Sal, whatever time you return, right here waiting for you. Give me a call to let me know that you are alright and if you need anything. I suppose I could do with the sleep anyway, in case Ali gets up. I just don't get any with you around."

I watched her dress, her lace underwear being placed over her tanned body, with her formal skirt and jacket topping it all off, concealing the precious gem that lay beneath. She clipped her hair up, pulling it into the formal style mostly demonstrated for work. It was still wet around the edges from the hot tub. She was the formal lawyer again. As she left the house, I heard the sound from the heels of her ankle boots clicking to her car, the burble of her new Porsche 911 resonating off the walls of the garage courtyard, as she drove away.

The seconds changed into minutes, the minutes created hours as I waited for her return. I used the time to carry out a few household chores, there were many associated with residing in a house like this. I then went to sleep for a while. Alice awoke around five-thirty, she was picked up by taxi and I spent some time working on a property deal that I was investigating for one of Sally's best clients. He owned a portfolio of warehouses in key locations, all suitable for future development, often located in areas adjacent to those which had been regenerated already.

Sally's phone was switched off, not unusual as she may well be dealing with an interview situation in a Police Station. What was unusual, was as the hours passed by, I had still heard nothing. I became slightly concerned, the concern gradually, but surely multiplying, like the breading of bacteria in a Petri Dish. It quickly covered the surface, and then deepened until it was taking over my health. It spread to my lungs; restricting the breath of life, attacking my heart; changing the speed and the rhythm, then finally murdering my brain; killing off any other thoughts. The hours passed by until they had summated to create a day. I called her office; they knew nothing of her location, Sal tended to work as a free spirit, reactive to the needs of her clients. This was a quality, which I was sure they often appreciated.

I called Mark and told the story and time of her departure. If anyone would know the location of Sal, it would be Mark. If anything in the underworld was occurring, it was likely that he would know about it, or would have heard a rumour floating around.

"Mark, she said it was her Little Sis that was in trouble. I have never met her, she does not say anything much about her family and likes to keep it private."

I was starting to feel panic, but trying hard to give the conversation a business-like, systematic approach.

He paused, seeming a little quiet; an element of concern was already lingering in his voice, being evident right from first picking up the phone. I suspected he had guessed the purpose of the call before he answered, and was likely to know what was going off.

"Why would you think that I know her sister? Leave it with me, I will find out if anything has happened. I will try the guys on the street and a few contacts at the police."

A day passed and there was no news, no call, the mobile remained switched off. Mark was also quiet, proving a little hard to get hold of. I suspected he was making himself a little illusive, knowing rather more than he was letting on. I tried all of the obvious routes to establish anything that had happened. I made contact with all of my clients, who had originated from Sal, as well as any known clients to me. All routes struck a blank. There was no news from the hospital, the police, or anyone else.

It was time after all to choose another route, to contact the police via a different approach. A person in their thirties, going missing, had not been of much interest to the police, especially not for the first few days. My route however, was to contact Detective Sergeant Armstrong. I remembered from my captivity that his approach to policing was hands on with people. I had no doubt that he had contacts with the underworld. He was also well known to Sal, I recalled their conversations while I was being held and his name had been mentioned on a few occasions, over the last few years. I made the call and he appeared a little more interested than the others. What was evident, was that she was not at the Police Station and had not visited the local police. I made it perfectly clear, that there would be something in it for him, if he could reveal any news. I was sure however, that with Mark also on the case, that I was probably not the only person making an offer, and any offer I made, as an outsider to such environments, may get ignored, unlike any contact from Mark. It was however worth a try, anything was.

Two days passed and my concern was growing in proportion, day by day, hour by hour, minute by minute and second by second, taking over my life. I travelled around when Antonie was looking after Alice, or if she was at school. I was not sure what I was looking for, but had to physically do something myself. The only positive news was that there was no bad news. At least with Alice's low level of understanding, there was no explaining about why Mum was not around to contend with. It also meant that Alice had no knowledge of the situation, so was not worrying, which would have fuelled my own concerns, that probably could not have expanded any further.

I was however going out of my mind, trying to concentrate on work and Alice, while busy thinking of any lead that I had. The two people whom I would have loved to contact, I could not; her illusive father and sister, as I had no details of either. Was she with them? What type of help was it that her sister actually needed? I had assumed that it was a legal situation, but it may not have been at all. Were they both in trouble? I had nothing to go on, no contact details, not even a vague location to try.

DS Armstrong did not appear to have any leads, but I was confident that he would be spreading the word around; after all, they appeared to get along. Armstrong must also have been close to retirement and soon gaining his pension. This I felt would be a nice little earner for him, also if he had to visit a location without a justifiable reason to give to his superiors, this would have been fine for him, he was on his way out, escaping from the new style of policing that he clearly hated.

All I could do was to keep going, keep hoping, and keep my spirits up. Falling down into depression was not an option, as it would not help Alice, or Sally. My frustrations were however growing and starting to spiral out of all control. It was more frustrating than my arrest for the explosion, eleven years earlier. I was free, but I knew somehow, that Sally was not. I was not sure if she was being detained, or if she was indeed with her sister or not, but there was no way that she would not make contact if there was a way. Maybe there was some great event, where someone needed to secure legal advice on hand twenty four hours a day, seven days a week. I hoped that they were looking after her in some hotel, just preventing her contact with the outside world, until the planned deed had been executed. Was it a simple form of risk management, to ensure that there were no possible leaks, until the deed had been completed? I did not know why I tried to convince my whole body of this invented story, it just gave me comfort that everything was alright and she would soon be at home. My brain was working overtime to reach this conclusion, to the point that it hurt, but it was the best option that I had, the best fantasy to indulge oneself in. It was all that I possessed.

The one thing that I could consider a certainty; was that Mark and a significant amount of the shady clients of Sally's, would be looking out for her. They respected her, admired her and many had her to thank for their freedom, after they had been caught in many a sticky situation. She always did her best to represent her clients, no matter what they had been accused of doing, or had indeed done. There were therefore a lot of people, those specialising in all types of crime, undertaking their own investigations. I strongly felt that her sister was the key to her location and indeed the whole crisis. If only I could locate her, I was sure that I could retrieve Sally.

I knew she was alive, I did not know how I knew, but I did. Any thoughts of her death, accident, or murder were soon quashed. We were close enough to often know what each other was thinking, to start laughing without any word being spoken, we would share a comical angle on some occurrence. I was therefore sure that if the worst had happened, I would have felt the pain, the suffering, the emotional feeling that would have accompanied the said act. The one thing that I was sure of was that I would never give up; it was a case of existing, surviving, until we were reunited.

I eventually got hold of the elusive Mark again.

"What can we do? I will do anything, I just want her back. I do not care how much it costs, or what risks I have to take. Do you know anything at all about her sister? I am sure she is the key to all of this."

"Look, I have told you before, I know what you are going through and I am working on it. I am on the case for both Sally and her sister. Remember the contacts I have, nothing happens around here without me, or my team knowing about it, or finding out about it. You are one of us, protected, shielded under the umbrella, which is where you will remain. I will work on this; all I need you to do is to help me when I ask and to carry on as normal, which in turn helps your little Alice and Sally."

I agreed, I did not feel like agreeing, but I did. Not that I did not want to help; I just did not want to carry on as if nothing had happened. Despite the reassurances from Mark that he was on the case, I remained troubled that he did not respond to my specific questions. He would never talk about the detail, no matter how much I tried to lead him into giving me a specific answer, instead he just continued to make reassuring noises, keeping me in the dark. There would be a reason behind this action, for that I was sure.

The police were the worst, not DS Armstrong, I was confident that he was looking into it, probably working alongside Mark. The rest of the police had concluded one of several things: That either Sally was fed up with me, gained a new partner and left, or she was fleeing from the pressure of having an autistic daughter. That she had made the decision to run away from the situation, life itself, or a combination of everything. I strongly did not believe their theories; I knew that they were not true. This also seemed to discount any mention of her sister in the proceedings. I did not care what they thought anyway, I had experienced enough of what they thought that I had done in the past. What mattered was what Mark could come up with, and to be fair he was right, if anyone could find something out, he was the person. What troubled me deeply however, was how long it was taking.

To make matters worse; if that was at all possible, since his call asking me to drive to Le Mans, I was now on that classic car run to France. The fog of concern was not just lingering over me as a mist, or drifting by; I was fully engulfed by the impermeable blanket. I felt helpless, but was continuing to go through the motions as Mark had been so insistent that I carried on. He said it was the right thing to do, but why? I was struggling to convince myself, but I knew that I must. Simply must. Mark said that it would help Sally. For Sally I was doing this, carrying on, for Sally. For Sally.

Chapter 10

The Classic Run

The near London traffic distracted my thoughts, it had to, the M25 near to rush hour, meant that for survival I had to have one thing clearly focussed in my mind; driving. The passing E-Type Jaguars had allowed my mind to wander into more pleasant things, just for a few fractions of a second, as my life drifted through my brain. Chapter by chapter it flashed by, reliving what had happened, how my career had turned out and how my life had evolved. There was only one thing that mattered at the current time however, that was Sally, her safety and us being reunited. If she wanted to go, she would have told me, we were open with each other, close, but understood that we were two individuals. We both had minds and lives of our own in addition to our time together.

My mind would not refocus from the fact that I did not want to be doing this; driving around, acting as if I was happily on the way to Le Mans, then going off on something resembling a holiday in Jersey. I knew that Alice would be safe and happy with Antonie, but with Sally missing, this was hard. I had to repeat in my own mind over and over again that it was what Mark had requested and anything I could do for him right now, I would. At the end of the day, there was nothing practical that I could do and I had my mobile phone firmly in my pocket, set to the most annoying, loudest tune in the menu, there was no way I was going to take any risks in missing a call.

I headed to the Channel Tunnel, pulling up at a McDonald's car park; this was to be a meeting point for the other club members. Already in the car park there was a Leaf Green Austin Healey Frogeye Sprite and two 1275cc MG Midgets from the early 1970's. I walked across to join them; the owners were studying a map spread out on one of the car bonnets. All three owners turned, they were older than I and greeted me with the usual, friendly welcome, which like-minded enthusiasts of the club tended to have.

Malcolm was the organiser of the convoy and accommodation at the destination; he had everything planned to minute detail. I would not have been surprised if he had just returned from a dummy run to Le Mans, just to check out that nothing had changed dramatically from the last time he visited, after all this would have been a full twelve months previous. As I knew all too well, a great deal could change in a moment, yet alone a full year.

He gave me the impression the first time that I set eyes upon him, as being someone who would have been an artist. He tended to wear flamboyant, brightly coloured clothes, and despite being in his late sixties, had long, flowing grey hair, tied back in a ponytail. I was sure that he had probably been good looking in his day and had lived life to the full when younger, back in the 1960's. In fact, I do not think he would have been out of place at a wild party now. I could visualise him at an all-night event, on the dance floor with a drink in one hand and something illegal to smoke in the other. I had known him for a good few years, meeting up at events such as this and having a few telephone calls in between. I had never enquired if he had any artistic talents, I just knew him for his engineering skills.

He was to be a risk to my intended actions on the trip. His organising ability and the preparation that oozed out of every pore, when combined with being one of the most naturally friendly and helpful people that anyone could ever meet, always someone who would be keen to help anyone out who was in need of assistance. I had a plan, a mission to complete. I was not just heading off to have an enjoyable time with my fellow club members. I knew that Malcolm would be the first person to try to keep us all on route, all heading in one direction together.

If anything faulted on my car, I was fully aware that he would have a full set of tools and spares on board, all of which he would readily offer to enable me to continue the journey. His car was also the same as mine, probably built only months apart. In fact they were pretty much identical, apart from minor cosmetic modifications and the colour. His car, like mine, was in immaculate condition. I worried that it would take a simultaneous fault with a common part on our cars, or an obscure component failure, to stop my car being quickly repaired. It would need to be something that he had not been able to stow away in the dark depths of the boot, which prevented him from being able to offer a solution to any problem. If all else failed, I also knew that he would have the passenger seat of his car on offer, as his wife was not at all interested in cars. He would usually travel on his own, but of course with his friends in the club making up the convoy.

Derek was just the opposite, early retired, tall, thin and totally conventional in appearance, with thinning dark hair. He tended to dress conservatively, often wearing a blue shirt and a dark tie. He was not dressed so formally today at the time of meeting, but I was sure that he would change into his usual attire at some point, probably prior to an evening meal when we were over the channel, in France. Again, he was also friendly, just in a different way to Malcolm. His car was clearly home restored, every little task proudly carried out by himself. The only difficulty was that this was not at all positive. He had welded, repaired and re-sprayed the car Damask Red in his garage, to shall we say, a standard that was not to mine. He had bundles of enthusiasm, and all credit to him for giving every little job a go. He just lacked the advanced skills that Malcolm possessed, or the ability to judge when his skills were running out. His car looked great from a distance, but as soon as you stood within a couple of metres of it, you could identify where he was not blessed with practical skills.

The third car was highly modified, both cosmetically and mechanically, it was obvious that it was driven rapidly, by someone with an interest in racing and fast driving. It was scruffy, with patches of rust bubbling through. The paint was a none standard metallic blue, the interior was modified and judging by the sound as he fired the engine up, the car was likely to be a little quicker than those of the rest of us. I had not met the owner, Paul, before; a rounded man, with short fair hair, in his mid-fifties. He again was friendly and had come along with his silver haired wife; Sandra of similar proportions. Their proportions were not the usual for the driver of an MG Midget, a little rounder than most, when considering the contortions needed to enter the car through the small doors. I suspected that he would be someone who may well break free from the pack given the opportunity of a stretch of clear road, and may find the sedate pace of the rest of us, a little too slow for him.

We ate breakfast prior to heading off in convoy, Malcolm as the lead to the Channel Tunnel terminus. Paul took the position at the rear, with him being the only person to have a willing assistant in the car to navigate if we were split up in the traffic. The one thing about ports, airports, and a terminus such as this, is the fact that to be fair, they are clearly signposted, so I was sure that we would all easily manage to arrive at our first destination at the same time.

I liked Malcolm a lot, his character always shone through, even with his over organised approach to events. Somehow it fascinated me that the two parts of his personality; organisation skills and his slightly eccentric ways, just never quite matched. He was someone who blew the theories of any narrow-minded person that believes in stereotypes straight out of the water. Derek was harmless, a nice bloke, just a little too formal for me, slightly stayed. He had more enthusiasm buried within him than he ever showed, it would have been good to see him relax and to let what was left of his hair down. This was something that I knew I would not see, but thought of what may happen if Malcolm slipped him something one day and he started to let go a bit.

Paul, I thought, may go it alone, the dynamic of his wife and interest in speed would be something that he would get carried away with. I was sure however that he would have a supply of interesting stories to tell, along the depths of the tunnel. I realised that asking him about the modifications to his car, would be responded to by the tales that only a true enthusiast could master. As for his wife, Sandra, she, too, seemed interested in the cars, and was clearly not someone who had joined just for the ride to France. She had made comments about those things called shops, so I was sure that at some point they would travel to the retail sector to spend hard earned cash.

We arrived at Folkestone after all having refuelled; it had taken time as we needed to use the same petrol pump, the only one that dispensed the higher octane unleaded fuel that our cars preferred. We joined the line, mainly consisting of holiday makers with their families, cars loaded up with cases, roof boxes stuffed with camping equipment and excited children looking around. To me the children were a bit of a pain, not that they were misbehaving particularly, or even that loud, but to my mind they were. I was used to a non-vocal little girl, who through no fault of her own, could not speak. The families waiting in line all had children chattering away, my mind drifted to think of what life would have been like without Alice's difficulties. Her autism prevented her from sharing her thoughts, emotions and feelings in a conventional manner. Would Ali have been here today if things had been different? Would she have had an interest in attending a trip like this, acting as my navigator, off on a foreign adventure, even if it was to be short? Then again, she would have been too concerned for where her mother had disappeared to if she had been alright. What would her interests have been? Where would her opinions, thoughts, skills and abilities have lain? Something that sadly, one will never know, knowledge that will never escape into the atmosphere to be set free, liberated, never to be revealed to the remainder of the world.

There were a number of other classic and performance cars, all forming the snake like line to the train. We boarded in line, a slow manoeuvre for us all. The boxes housing some type of component of the train protruded from the floor, not something that could be taken quickly, otherwise risk of damage to the underside of the cars would be the result. Not a real problem for the three of us with standard cars, but Paul's modified car was lowered. People behind our convoy were starting to get impatient by our slow progress, with Paul still bringing up the rear by an increasing margin.

We arrived in Calais, deciding to stop for coffee and a snack before our drive to the hotel in Grand camp-Maisy. We had arranged to spend two days heading to Le Mans, to take in some of the sights, after all, when travelling this distance it would have been a shame not to make the most of the miles and see a few parts of France. Derek, Paul and to some extent, Malcolm were all interested in the Second World War history of the northern French coast, they wished to see some of the D-Day landing sights and German defences. It was decided to try to stick to the coastal roads; they would be far more interesting than the main roads anyway. Heading along the seafront was something that was always of interest to me anyway. I had not taken too much notice of the planned itinerary beyond the first day, as my trip was to be shorter than planned, cut tragically short by mechanical disaster, resulting in my departure to Jersey.

Arrangements of meeting places were formulated in case we got separated and we left for our first section of the journey. As we stood up, I made sure that I was the last to head out of the door, placing my sunglasses in my pocket. We drove off, heading along the D940. I was at the back, Malcolm taking the lead. I called Malcolm as soon as we were heading along the coast.

"Malc, I have gone and left my sunglasses in the café, I am heading back as they are my decent ones. I will catch you up somewhere near the cliffs of Cap-Blanc-Nez."

"You, Pratt, you are not capable of leaving a café on your own, next time I will leave the table last. It's like looking after a party of school kids."

Malc laughed; finding my inability to take care of myself amusing.

I headed back out of sight, pulling up on the coast road. The breeze was flowing off of the sea. The tide was coming in, turning white on the breakwaters. I turned the car around, waiting near to some scrubland. All was quiet so I lifted the bonnet, taking a screwdriver and the faulty condenser out of the boot of the car. It had been packed for a moment such as this, during my final preparations. I pulled off the distributer cap, removed the good condenser and replaced it with the spare one, known to be faulty. I got back in the car, turned the ignition and pulled the starter button. The car fired into life with a slight misfire, as I started off again. The misfire got progressively worse from an occasional jerk, accompanied with a loss of power, to being totally unable to run.

The plan was complete. The car was disabled, ready for my unfortunate end to the trip. I was disappointed as deep down I would have loved to have continued with the trip, but for me, that was never the plan. I got out of the car, fitting the hood and shutting the side screens. As I turned around, a leaf-green Frogeye Sprite was heading towards me; Malcolm. Great, this was all that I needed; the most friendly, helpful person that you would ever wish to meet. The ideal club member, always there to assist had appeared. Not only did he have those great mechanical skills, but that endless supply of tools and spare components. This was all I wanted. I had arranged with Mark Daniels that this is where the car would be left, as secured as it could be, with me getting a taxi and flying into Jersey. I knew that Malcolm would diagnose and fix the car.

"What is up now, trouble? I really cannot leave you for a moment!"

"I lost power, had a misfire and she died."

"Come here, I'll see what I can do."

Malcolm, armed with tools soon located the problem, a faulty condenser and fitted a spare that he just happened to have in the car. He pulled the starter and she burst into life once more, as smooth as before.

"There are a lot of faulty condensers around at the moment a bad batch of cheap imitations came into the country."

We were off again, heading to check into the hotel at Grand camp-Maisy. What was I to do? All I could do was to thank Malcolm and follow. I could hardly say that I had deliberately fitted the knowingly faulty part, so that I could leave the trip, abandon my car along the road, that it would then be picked up by a recovery truck a few hours later as I flew on to Jersey. Malcolm had done his hero of the moment, good turn as usual, an exemplar yet again, of what the club was about. I could hardly tell him to piss off, as I wanted to break the car again. The wonderful natured bloke had unintentionally done exactly what I did not want. I was now going to be late, maybe running a day off schedule for the transfer as I knew he would stick to me like glue, to ensure that I had no further mishap.

I sent Mark a text, saying that there was a delay and I was staying over, asking if there was any news. The phone soon bleeped back, ordering me to make it early tomorrow.

Malcolm and I checked into the hotel, I was the brunt of a few jokes for a while. Paul and Sandra had already arrived, with Derek not far behind us, after stopping to check out a monument to the French and British Marines in the war. The cars were all parked in a line in the car park, causing much interest to other guests, locals and staff who were on their smoking breaks.

I had not taken much notice of the hotel when the arrangements for the trip were made, as I was not intending to make it as far as the overnight halt. It was contemporary, in fact the chosen venue was a rather surprisingly modern choice for a group of classic car enthusiasts, most of which were beyond middle age. Externally it was finished in different coloured renders, with the various blocks ranging in height, from single up to five storeys. A central courtyard housed an open air swimming pool, with children playing with a multi-coloured ball. Parents sat drinking around the edge, dressed in swimwear to soak up the sun's rays. Again, I was reminded at how different having children in the normal circumstances could be. Not to mention that they were together as a family. With Alice it would have been a case of being in the pool, becoming a rock for her to cling to. My hair would be grabbed like seaweed trailing from the rock, with Alice grasping firmly, so as not to be swept away by the tide created by a passing swimmer. I was not one for swimming either, being someone with a natural tendency to sink.

Inside, I had never stayed anywhere quite like it. The modern image was illustrated to the extreme, including within the bedrooms. The floor was wood effect rather than carpet, with all walls and furniture being a minimalist, almost clinical shade of pure white. The only contrast was the bedding and curtains in a dull shade of brown that was almost straying across the border into grey. The item that seemed rather strange to me initially was the fact that I had a kitchenette in the room. I thought I was in a hotel, not a studio used as student accommodation. On further investigation, it was found to be a cross between a hotel and serviced apartments. It was to be a new experience, although only for one night. All of the usual hotel services such as breakfast were all extra, additional to the room package. It was however new and clean, just not quite what I had imagined.

We retired to the bar to discuss the following day's events. I was pleased to have a drink; it helped to calm my frustrations regarding both Sally and the failed breakdown. I had planned my events for the day, but they were not to be shared. Derek and Malcolm planned to head to Bayeux to view the Bayeux Tapestry and the Eleventh Century Norman Cathedral Notre Dame. Paul and I agreed to explore the town on foot in the morning, while Sandra looked around any shop she could find. We were to all meet in the afternoon after heading south via the Chateau and museum at Balleroy. I would have loved to look at the Gothic cathedral, but that way I had no chance of escape. I needed to do the opposite to the mechanical genius. Malcolm passed around a brochure about Balleroy for the afternoon adventure. Describing how the place was turned into a hot air balloon museum, by a multi-millionaire American newspaper person, who had been the first to cross America by this unconventional form of transport.

"Look at the gates they are huge, but set in a low wall. How pointless is that? You could stride right in, not to mention look straight in when you passed by." I observed.

"Not like your bloody wall and blocked up gates, you want to see his place, he has almost got a roof over the garden to stop people in passing hot air balloons looking in. I don't know how that Malcolm Forbes did it. I'm a Malcolm and had a paper round and earned only a few shillings."

"It must have been a bloody big round, Malc."

We all dined, I then went for a walk to the harbour, wanting some solitude. Usually, I would have stayed with the others, but wanted some time to escape. Some time to think, some time to be alone. I walked along the marina, once a busy fishing port and having played its part in the Normandy landings. Now there was a new marina, full of pleasure craft, with the odd small fishing boat bobbing around near to the harbour wall. I looked back at the restaurants with water frontage. They were busy, locals and tourists dining out and having a few drinks. Mainly couples, couples enjoying their partners company and the atmosphere of the setting sun, on a warm summer evening. I however was alone, the sight of the couples cutting in and twisting my situation, as I wondered where Sally was, if she was alright and what was happening with her sister. I saw a glimpse of Paul and Sandra enjoying absorbing the atmosphere, ramming it home that even within the party of club members, there was someone in the situation that I was trying not to think about.

I turned to face the sea, the sun now a burning bright orange above the movement of the waves, glistening and reflecting off the surface of the water. The sound in the background of voices grew fainter, replaced by the movement of ropes, their clanking against the metal masts of the sailing boats in the gentle breeze. The sun faded lower and lower on the horizon, matching my mood, as it drowned and died beneath the sea. The darkness gained intensity, gathering its anger as the temperature dropped. I continued to feel worse as I looked out to sea, the time passing as the sound of the waves and ropes on masts became more intense. I looked to the sky, stars and moonlight had replaced the sun, knowing that somewhere under that great, vast sky, beneath the sparkling crystal stars lay Sally. Where; I did not know, but she was out there, somewhere. She had been beneath the same setting sun and was now looked down upon by the same stars, enwrapped in the same sky. But where was she? Could she see it? Was she feeling the same? The air temperature dropped further as I continued to watch, taking in the sadness of the mood, almost enjoying it, as I did not want to be happy for a while, not without Sal.

I walked back to the hotel, taking a walk to the car first, spending a few moments sitting in the sparse interior. The others were now all safely in the bar, where I was sure, they would now remain for a few hours. It was safe to make an adjustment again, something that would not easily be spotted. I grasped a bottle of natural spring water from the passenger foot well and climbed out of the car. Looking around there was nobody. The cars were all parked together in a corner of the car park, reversed towards a wall. I squeezed between the wall and the back of the car, turned the chrome fuel filler cap and poured the water into the small, almost empty, petrol tank, then replaced the cap.

The following morning I called Antonie to check on how the little mischief had been, I waited for her to be picked up for school before making the call. I knew, and understood all too well, that before the pickup, Antonie would have her hands rather full. Running around, attempting to dress, a disappearing, fast moving little person, who is climbing all over the furniture, probably jumping up and down while pointing at the CD player for the next track takes skill. I was sure Antonie would also have done a far better styling job of her hair, than I ever could master.

"Hi, how has she been, did you get any sleep?"

"She has been great. Full of fun, bouncing around and slept through to almost five o'clock."

Reassured that the mischief was alright, I continued with the day's events.

We all met for the optional extra breakfast, of typical continental style, then checked out of the hotel. Derek and Malcolm headed off to Bayeux, Paul, Sandra and I leaving the cars at the hotel, then heading to explore the settlement on foot.

There was a street market, mainly selling fresh fish; it appeared Sandra was interested in anything retail, even down to a fish market, but then there was the French atmosphere to absorb. We wandered off to see the World Peace Statue. Not having been here before, I was taken aback by the amount of references to the war, the number of gun towers facing out to the sea, intended to stop the British and American forces from invading the invaded country. I learnt that the severe, almost cold, ferocious gun batteries were part of Hitler's Atlantic wall. They were designed to be impregnable, a number of cannons were still present, restored to mark this dark part of history. Whether restoration of them was the right thing to do, was a different matter. Was this a reminder of where society had been, in its dark past and where it must never return to in the future? The total waste of life, as well as resources, combined with suffering, both for those fighting and the ones remaining at home. Did it celebrate the dark period of history, adding to glorify war and the so called honour, of making the ultimate sacrifice for one's country? After all, the fact that the situation arose and became the slaughter that it did, was a demonstration of complete failure. The failure was not only to prevent a dictator, but failure to stop the brainwashing in its tracks and prevent the great loss of life on all sides. It was a government and society failure, on a massive, world wide scale.

Alternatively, were they there for tourism, a sight to be seen, to make money out of the death and suffering, while educating the people of today? To me there existence was one thing, but anything being restored as a memorial was something different, maybe they should have been allowed to gradually deteriorate and die, or be converted into other uses.

I looked at a street that led down to the sea, gradually sloping down. From a distance, the sea could be viewed as the ultimate destination for the road, and it appeared that the road's main purpose was to enter the water. It would have been attractive, but was rather spoilt and cluttered by overhead cables, running in different directions, resembling a tangled web. I thought about driving the car down there, to take a photograph in the street with the sea in the background.

We had spent time walking around and I needed an excuse to try to start the car, I was already almost twenty-four hours behind schedule. I simply could not wait until we were to leave to meet the others, heading south in the afternoon. Mark had clearly been forced to reschedule once already, it could not be allowed to happen again. There were probably several people involved in this and the recovery truck may also be standing by. I needed to perform for Mark, under the current circumstances this desire was amplified; I had a lot resting on Mark and his contacts.

"Paul, I am nipping back and bringing the car. I want a photograph of an old street with the car parked on it and the sea in the background. Maybe a potential one for the cover of the club magazine, see you shortly."

"I'll come with you and get mine, too. Sandra will be too busy trying to look as if she has been on a London shopping expedition to Oxford Street, or even to New York. One day she may even remember that we can never get everything in the car for the return journey. Last year, we spent a fortune posting half of the so called bargains back home."

We soon returned to the hotel car park, I knew that there was not much petrol in the small tank, and the water content would prevent the car from making it. It would however start, being run from the fuel contained within the carburettors, fuel filter, pump and fuel lines. I climbed in the car, pulled out the choke, turned the key and pulled the starter button. The car burst into life, I let the car run for a few moments to clear the good petrol from the fuel lines, and then started to move off, as soon as I did so, the car spluttered, faltered then stopped.

Paul and I looked under the bonnet. We carried out the usual checks on the ignition system, finding not surprisingly, that there was a good, strong, spark at the plugs. We then checked that fuel was reaching the carburettors, which of course it was. There was nothing to indicate that anything was wrong, which was hardly surprising, as there was no fault with the car for anyone to find. An hour passed, it became evident that the problem would not be found. In fact, even if the guru Malcolm had been with us, he was unlikely to have found any fault, although he may have investigated more thoroughly. It had not rained, we had not been through water, or filled up with petrol at different pumps from each other, so water in the fuel would not have been a suspicion.

"Look, you two go on. Go and meet the others, I will call for the breakdown assistance and get the car back to England. It has obviously developed a fault. If the recovery guy can spot a problem, I will call you and meet up at Le Mans. If you lot start messing around, you will not reach Le Mans in time to look around the pits before the activity commences."

"I can ask Malcolm to come over, he may fix it and we could still catch the first race. We can miss out on Balleroy."

"No it's not fair, Paul. You know Malcolm he will end up missing racing to look at the car. Go to meet them, explain and send my apologies. I may well be up and running later, so see you at Le Mans yet."

They left, I felt relieved. The car was immobilised, located in a safe, but secluded area of the car park. After all the car did not lock, no door locks were ever fitted. For anyone to access the car, all they needed to do, was to slide open a side screen and reach through the opening. They would then feel the metal lever, which served the purpose of the internal door handle.

I sent a text to Mark, to say that unfortunately I was not going to make it to Le Mans, as the car had broken down at the hotel in Grand camp-Maisy. This was the news that I was sure he had been longing for, waiting an additional day to hear, and frequently checking the phone for any missed text. I made my arrangements from the hotel, to be picked up by taxi and travel to Saint-Malo. From there, I would catch the ferry to Jersey, an island retreat that I loved and we had visited on many occasions. Accommodation had already been arranged, prior to the start of the trip. I had already missed one night of my booking. I was supposed to have entered France by car, leaving without the car, later in the same day. Then again, that is classic car ownership for you. Even breakdowns do not always go to plan. The cars are easy and cheap to fix compared with the new technology of the modern car, yesterday had proved they could be all too easy to repair.

I finalised the arrangements to head to Saint-Malo and had a wander down to the new marina, while waiting to be picked up. On my return to the hotel at the agreed time for the taxi, a black Renault Espace bearing French registration plates, pulled up in the parking space next to my car, which was earlier vacated by Paul and Sandra. The driver got out. Tall, slim, dark haired, with well-tanned skin. He was wearing a black shirt and beige casual trousers. His dark tinted glasses, protecting his eyes from the glare of the sun. He opened my passenger door, leant into the car, closed it back up, re-entered his car and left. He carried out the whole operation quickly and swiftly, not having to look how to open my car. It was one quick, smooth move and he was gone. He left the car park as calmly and as casually as he arrived. Anyone not familiar with the car would have struggled to gain entry, looking for the door handle. Not this man; he either knew classic cars, had completed his homework, or had placed a package into my car on a previous occasion during a similar run.

The whole operation would have gone unnoticed to anyone, the size of the seven seat people carrier, completely obscuring my tiny car. I was waiting for something to happen and hardly noticed myself, so a bystander would not have registered the action. If they had, they would have assumed he was accessing his own car, expecting a struggle, or fumbling around if it had been an unauthorised entry, failing that, some degree of force, or hesitance. The manoeuvre was so confidently executed. I had left the car keys safely at reception, for the recovery vehicle to collect, explaining about the breakdown and its departure to England.

There was now of course something in my car, something placed within, something unknown, in fact, and I did not even see any object in the hands of its courier. It was not large, or heavy. I wanted to return to the car, to look inside, the temptation was great; wanting to know what was being transported into the country in my car. Wondering what it was that could not have been posted into England, or brought in by hand. Why did this entire act need to be staged to avoid something? I guessed that it must be drugs, but I had no evidence, I did not want evidence. It was something I chose not to know about, but it helped me to live my lifestyle. Why Mark paid me so much for this, I did not comprehend. Surely, this was something that anyone could do for a few pounds? They would enjoy the trip at the same time. I was paid well for this type of activity, not to mention the recovery cost, which would not be cheap. My car of course did not have locks, so could have been accessed by anyone, at any time, so as far as I was concerned, I was safe if anything went wrong. There was no evidence that I had any knowledge of this and that was the way it would stay.

There was temptation, but not enough for me to risk returning to the car, looking for something that had been added, risking being seen after passing the keys to reception, risk of having my finger prints added to whatever the mystery item was. The risk was just too great, despite feeling inquisitive. I stayed well clear of the car, something I had always done in the past. Each time it got harder though, the naturally inquisitive nature of the human, that had allowed mankind to adapt, invent and develop, was getting harder to resist. There was the question as to what I would do, or if I would continue, if I established what was going on and it was not something that I approved of. This again would place me in a difficult position, especially the one with Mark.

I kept away, remaining clear from the car, as I waited for my transport to Saint-Malo to arrive. As the taxi appeared, behind it was a silver van with curtain sides, on English registration plates. As it turned the corner, the sign written sides came into view; 'Car Transportation Services'. I was pleased that my little car was getting the service, often only reserved for the prestigious Marques. I also noted the containment; it formed a total shield from prying, inquisitive eyes.

I arrived at Saint-Malo, the grey granite buildings and walls looking stern and forbidding on first sight. The taxi driver spoke perfect English and told me that the town was once a fortified island in the middle ages. It controlled the estuary and the open sea beyond. It had been notorious for fierce pirates, who could not be controlled by anyone. It now appeared to be a lively place, full of bars, restaurants and shops. There was however, no time or inclination to explore. I left the taxi and joined the ferry for Jersey.

Chapter 11

Sisters!

Sally arrived at her little sister's penthouse apartment, parking in the car park below the building. Everything was more than a little familiar to Sally, after all, it was the penthouse that she had sold to her sister, when moving to her current gothic residence a good few years ago now. She entered the lift, to be quickly transported to the top floor, wondering exactly what she would find, what trouble her little sister had become involved in this time.

Emily was two years younger than Sally and very different, she was daring in a different type of way. Where Sally had used her intelligence to enter the field of law, proving to be a very successful partner in her chosen field of work, Emily had taken a less academic and more brutal, down to earth approach to her career. Despite being a young female in a man's world, she had chosen from a young age to follow in her father's footsteps, something that her father had strongly discouraged. It had taken a few years for him to accept that she would follow him into his business. She had however, proved her worth and was a great asset, in a totally different kind of way.

Emily was taller than her Sister, and a little bigger built, differing in her appearance, significantly. Emily liked to visit the gym, taking pride in herself that she was fitter and stronger than many men, but still in a feminine, toned, rather than muscular way. She was attractive, but not as pretty as her sister. Her original dark hair having been concealed since she was a young teenager, it never over the years had ever been revealed beneath what was now considered by everyone, to be her natural blonde hair. She was intelligent, probably more intelligent, just expressed her talents in a different way, a more cunning, calculated way. She also mixed with many of Sally's clients, in many cases they were her friends. She had not settled down like Sally and had always strongly failed to understand her sister's new approach to life. She had dated various boyfriends over the last few years, always choosing the ones with an image that was bad, tough, and muscular, the type that could win a fight. These were regularly dispersed by a move to the other extreme, choosing an attractive girlfriend, in periods when she was fed up with male company, having been let down by the latest tough guy.

Despite her intelligence and well executed running of the family business with her father, she was now in some kind of trouble. The two sisters were reasonably close; Sally had merely decided to keep the two parts of her life separated by the Great Wall of China, so that they did not drift together. She did not have a problem with her sisters, or fathers, approach to life; she just decided that both professionally and personally she wanted a divide. Especially now that she was in the relationship of her dreams, what she had wanted from being a little girl and now had Alice to consider. Her approach of living the two lives was strange by most people's standards, but it was what she wanted.

There was something that they both had in common; if either sister desired something, they ensured that it was precisely what they got; compromise was not an option for consideration. They both had determination and strong character, neither being afraid of coming forward, a clear result of their upbringing. At some point Sally would bring together her inherited family, with her chosen partner and daughter, but to date, she had wanted a divide, for a reason better known to her. Pete understood and supported that, choosing in his normal laid back approach, that she must have a reason and it was her choice as an individual. That when the time was considered right, she would integrate the two parts of her life, although Pete did not realise there was already an intersection and there had been since before they first met.

Sally reached the door and entered the hallway. The modern, minimalist, design and furniture was a stark contrast to her own dwelling. Her sister looked worried, concerned, older than her years, her eyes looking deep set and lined, not herself at all. On the other hand, she did not appear to be in immediate danger, as she had thought was the case, when coming over to the rescue.

"So Emily, how are you? What trouble have you got yourself into this time? It better be good, we had got Alice to sleep early, so I was about to have a rather enjoyable evening."

"Is that all you two ever think about?"

"Well, you have obviously never found the right man then Emily, or is it girl at the moment?"

"That's all part of the problem, Sal. Thanks for coming, it is complicated and I do not want Dad to find something out. We are in trouble, not just me, that is why I got you here. It was important that your Pete did not find out."

Emily poured two large drinks and sat on the edge of the sofa, rocking forward towards her. Sally looked around the room, noticing the new modern art original, that had been added to the wall. The minimalist decor failed at one point; the walls. Some rooms were covered, almost cluttered, in modern art paintings, gathered from around Europe. Many, to Sally, looked like random splashes of paint on canvas, but had all been carefully crafted to give that impression, concealing their hidden meaning, prior to being sold to collectors such as Emily, for significant sums of money. Sally was not feeling very patient, not yet hearing anything that could not have waited until the morning.

"Well then, Sis, I am waiting and so is someone back home."

"You must not go home. You need to stay here with me; you are in trouble too, besides I need your brains for this one. A different, more cultured approach."

"I can give you that in the morning, Em, now just get on with the explanation will you, especially how this latest trouble involves me."

"I split with Delroy, he is still working for the business, but is on his merry little way as he is double crossing us. Dad always trusted him, he knows too much. He was after a cut of something that your beloved is going to bring into the country. He knows about a package that is coming in on one of the classic car runs, I know what it is but I am sure that you two don't. In fact, Dad has not asked him yet but wants him to head out to Le Mans, something to do with a race. Delroy was going to expose you two. So I stopped him. He got what he deserved alright, I thought it had worked, but then last week you got that tough guy; Lee Field off in court. There is history and rivalry between them, goes back a few years. Word has it he is freaked out about it. Lee once put him in hospital. It has resurrected his mission and is now after both of us. I am scared what he will do, but I think I know what he is plotting."

"Em, all we have to do then is tell Dad, he will take care of the problem. I fail to see the difficulty. It is nothing that Dad, you and I can't handle between us. This is the type of thing that you do day in, day out for a living."

"There is more to it. The package is drugs to be sold via the door staff. It is a normal situation. The problem is after the drugs have been moved."

"Dad will just change the arrangements; anyway there is nothing that could be pinned on my Pete. He will drive over in one of the old cars when Dad asks him. The car will breakdown, it will be picked up by a recovery van, the car will not be locked, as it does not have them fitted, so anyone can place something in the car at any point from the breakdown, to its arriving back at our house. The police would not be able to do a thing, and if they were planning something, old Armstrong will find out and tell us."

"I'm just scared he knows about the big one that is to follow. It is not exactly illegal, but he could just make things a little awkward. I am purchasing a Red Diamond and have already sold it on. It is a bit like the back-to-back property deals that your Pete does, just with a rare, famous stone instead. Dad is getting Pete to move it. All he will do is transport it a few miles across Jersey. The problem is that it is already in Jersey, and being sold to someone in Jersey. If that gets intersected, we have a real problem. I am getting it cheap, real cheap. A former banker, who has lost out big time in the recession and has a habit to feed, is selling it. I have sold it to someone on the island, if they find out it is a few miles down the road and not coming over from Brunei like I told them, we will be in trouble. Not to mention that I am selling for a figure, several times higher than I am buying at. It is to someone who is big time. Bigger than us, has the money and power to destroy anyone, if the deal gets exposed it would be me that gets converted into ash. Just do not tell anyone that you are here, not even Pete, you know what Delroy is like at mobile phone hacking, he will know everything we say."

"What? I am not going missing! Not disappearing without telling Pete and Alice."

"You must. Trust me, you must. Del is after you for getting Lee off, you are safe here. If you are out of the equation, missing, it will give our contacts something to do looking for you. News will soon spread around, turning people against Delroy as he made no secret of his annoyance when Lee walked free from court. Lee will then take care of Delroy and there will be no risk to anyone including Pete moving the Red Diamond. Three days, that is all that it will take. After then the Red Diamond will be moved, people with more muscle and anger than concern of the consequences will have taken care of Del."

“You are putting Pete at risk. He is to deliver the jewel across the island, a hot deal; meanwhile his car is delivering coke from France to England in large quantities.”

“Exactly why you need to stay here, then the risk is eliminated. Dad will give Pete reassurances that you are alright, but not over the phone and that everything is under control. Just trust him to do that.”

“Pete has no idea that Mark is my Dad, no idea at all. He has no idea that you are my sister. He just thinks I am a lawyer, who mixes with a few criminal clients. He believes that I simply choose not to have much to do with my family for some personal reason. Not that he does know my Dad already and did before he even met me.”

“You mean to say, Sal; he has no idea why he is under the umbrella? Why Dad pays him silly amounts of money for odd jobs, to support his granddaughter and lifestyle. The grandchild that he has always wanted and protects in the only way he knows, by sharing his money, as he is too fucking scared for all his front and bulk to come to terms with his soft side and Alice’s problem. He just cannot cope with it. His dream may not ever turn around and call him granddad. So he decides that if no one knows Alice is his granddaughter, she would not be calling him granddad anyway. The man, who has put people in hospital and probably killed, cannot cope with a little situation called autism when it is so close to him. He is too afraid to face the issue. What is your beloved going to say when you reveal all of this after over ten years? Ten long years, you have sat back, letting him think that you have had a problem in your childhood that you do not want to face. All along there has been no abuse, no problems, no fall outs, just a twenty stone block of muscle that like you cannot face the facts. Then before Alice, you came crying to me that Pete thought that you were just a fellow professional like him, a lawyer, not part of a family that controls the underworld for the region.”

“What is the sudden concern, Em? Why the sudden interest in my life? Why does it matter to you, what I have led

Pete to believe, as I thought our world would have been too much for him, putting him off when we first met? There has just never been the right moment to integrate you all, not after keeping my life and family divided for so long. You are usually too busy with the clubs, drugs, stolen gear and threatening to throw the companies weight around to bother. Why have you not told Dad, or got him to take care of Del? I want nothing to do with this. Tell Dad to cancel the run. Stuff your Red Diamond; I am off home, to bed, to have the great time that I intended to have. To pretend none of this has happened and to tell Dad, Armstrong and Lee that Del is after me. You are not in danger at all, if the planned events, get unplanned and do not happen, neither is Pete. It is only Del after me, for doing my job, legally and legitimately."

Sally got up, turned around and walked towards the door, ready to turn her back on her sister, angry at what she had said, angry at what had been planned for Pete. If nothing happened, than there was nothing to expose and all she had to do was to be careful. A simple call from the car on the way home, to tell Detective Sergeant Armstrong that Delroy had a grudge, as well as one to Lee Field, then both sides of the law would be covered. If he was hacking her phone, his exposure should tame his intentions. If all else failed, then her father would step in. As for Emily, then if she was not so greedy, the deal would be a simple, legitimate, purchase and sale, acting as a shop, an everyday retail act.

Emily started to cry, clearly genuinely upset. Her tough image had faded and left, fled from her body, something that never happened even in the toughest situation. She had no problem with sacrificing someone's life if they got in the way of her image, or one of her games. This was an approach that was hardly ever needed, as setting people in the underworld against each other, employing careful co-ordination and a few well-placed messages with the right person, usually prevented the need for direct intervention, that and financially looking after the right people. This time it was different, her usual blindness to reality and normality was not there. She wiped the tears from her face, and looked up at Sally shouting across the hallway.

"You are wrong. The first few words that you spoke were wrong, OK? I have found love, I do know what it is like to love and be loved, what it is like to want to spend the rest of your days with someone. I want to spend the day in bed. I want to spend almost every waking and living hour with someone."

Sally turned around; hurt that her little sister was hurting so much, concerned that she was letting something upset her to this extent. She was shocked and amazed at this outburst. This was not the tough Emily usually displayed. She turned, paused and faced Emily, who had thrown herself head first on the sofa. Sally's thoughts then performed a U-turn, making her own conclusion from the conversation, she shouted across at her, being unable to contain her anger and frustrations.

"So you have gone and fucking done it then. Fallen in love with the double crossing fucking Delroy, who is stitching the whole family up and you are fucking well joining in, playing his game against us all. Well you will get what you deserve, as I am telling Dad. I am not having you put my family at risk and yourself as well. I wondered why you were not going to take direct action against him."

"Sal, no! No! No! Sal, you have it all wrong. I got rid of Del as I found what you have, began to understand what you have, which is all I always wanted. It's not that Del, its Sophie. I love Sophie. I'm marrying Sophie. We are planning the wedding, we are happy together. We are as happy as we could ever be. Del said he was to tell Dad. I just do not know how he will take it. He is obsessed with wanting grandchildren, absolutely obsessed and you two have made it clear that you will not have any more, despite your obsession with sex. Now I am not to have any, we will be together until our dying days, I know that, but he will not like it. He has one granddaughter, one that he is terrified of admitting to, not that he does not love her. He wants to protect and support her. He is just too damn scared of her condition to get close to her. He loves her, but distances himself, not that you have given him much choice. He was relying on me to produce a child that he was not scared of. Now I have let him down. He just will not be able to accept it. You know how tough he thinks that he is. He knows that I am bisexual; he has no problem with it. He just thinks I will end up with a bloke, but I am not, if I went anywhere near one, or was artificially inseminated it would be cheating on Sophie. That is how I feel, how I always will feel and Del is to tell him. It needs to be me. I am to tell him, after you have come clean with Pete. The family, all of us need to stop pretending and tell the ones that we love how we feel and introduce who is bloody well whom."

"I am still confused. How about a little accident or something for Del? The sooner the better, direct intervention, that way there will be no problem for any of us."

"That is what all of this is arranging, keeping you two clear, keeping Sophie and I quiet until the moment is right, while letting someone else take care of Del. It must not be us, as he will not be in this alone. If we do anything to him, one of us, or both of us, gets in the shit from whoever he has told. My way lets him get taken care of by someone else. The exposure will be on him. That way the family are all in the clear, every single one of us, so is the business. It will be just a rogue employee that gets himself in trouble with someone else. Dad remains happy until we can break the news gently. If all this came out to Pete after all of these years, how do you think that he would react? What about the way that you have mislead him? How he thinks that all your time is spent representing clients, not involved with us in the business as well. That would look great, Sal, really great. Surely it is for you to tell him as soon as you can, when this is all over. Let him know what happens, what your family get up to and whom you are. At the same time it is for me to tell Dad about Soph, so we can all be united, take the risk on what he thinks, he needs us, and Pete idolises you."

“I will stay. You are sure that you have all of this right and that Dad will contact Pete, to say that I am OK as soon as he can?”

“Yes, if Delroy is phone hacking you and Pete like I suspect he is, any contact from you will be monitored. Everyone must think that you are in trouble, that way you will be the focus. I do not know whom Del is in with, but it is someone, probably someone who wants to move into our area and take over the clubs. It has to be someone who does not respect the family. It will soon be put to rest without any direct action. He is the only person stupid enough to try this. They will go away as soon as he is no longer around.”

Sally stayed at her sisters, they poured a few drinks and reflected on how their lives had evolved, shared secrets that they were both holding and their feelings about the situations that they were both now in. They however did not let the guard down; believing that Delroy Patterson was now plotting against them both for no reason apart from doing their job, or exposing their true feelings. These simple everyday acts, being something that so often could be a major source of trouble, in thousands of lives throughout the world.

Chapter 12

Best Intentions

A day passed by, Sally and Emily spending their time chatting as sisters do, making the most of the situation. Emily periodically left the apartment for business purposes, but never leaving her big sister unattended for long. There was no sign out there of Delroy, but Emily was sure he would be around, looking out for the sisters and Pete. She was convinced that Sally would be the main focus of his attention at that moment in time.

The news was spreading that Sally was not around, that she had disappeared and not been seen. Pete had started to make desperate calls to the police, Armstrong, hospitals and of course to Mark. Emily was not impressed with her father. She thought that he should have gone straight round to Pete, to set his mind at rest, let him know that the love of his life was safe and well. Her father disagreed, he was insisting on waiting a day, just to get Pete to make the appropriate calls, the enquiries, those that only someone desperately worried and upset would make. He believed that the calls must be genuine, straight from the depths of the heart, with a full set of expressive emotions, those only someone who is frantically trying to locate a missing loved one could make. Emily saw his point; she understood that he was doing this with all the best intentions for Sally. She did however have concern for

Pete, now that she was with Sophie, she understood for the first time what it would feel like and the torture that his soul must be feeling. Prior to meeting Sophie, Emily was harder, expressing fewer emotions, but along with her true feelings for another person outside of the family, empathy had also arrived in her life.

Emily convinced Sally that their father had been to visit Pete, to reassure him that she was safe, that she could not talk but was staying at her sisters, helping her out with something that needed her constant attention. Sally knew that Pete would understand this and not question, taking the approach that she would contact him when she was ready and able. That he would adopt the same attitude as he had for all of these years with regard to her family.

The sisters were in the kitchen, preparing food in the room that had changed drastically since Sally had owned it. The new, gloss, cherry wood units were smooth, shiny and minimalist, mounted with black granite worktops and multi-coloured glass splash backs which were close to forming a piece of artwork. Modern art was peppered around the walls, feature coloured LED lights were strategically placed around. They were chatting as they prepared dinner, a task that they had not carried out together for a number of years. There was a sudden noise in the hallway. It was an instantly familiar sound to Sally, recognisable from when she owned the apartment. It was the front door opening. Sally jumped, looked around, she felt tense, concern replacing blood and flowing through her body, flooding every pore. She grasped the sharp knife that she was using to prepare vegetables, sliding it down to the side of her leg. Emily took no notice, not even appearing to have heard the sounds, let alone acknowledge them by taking any action. There was a clatter of shoe heals in the hallway, she turned to look at Emily without uttering a word. The kitchen door started to swing open, as someone was entering the room.

The sisters looked around, Sally firmly grasping the knife in her hand, her grip and body becoming tense, her knuckles turning white with the intensity of her grip. Her heart started to race, her father and sister may be used to such situations, but she was not. The knife was well concealed between her leg and the kitchen unit, as the door to the kitchen diner swung open. A tall, dark, beautiful lady, of mixed black race stood in the doorway, dressed in a black dress. Her hair tied back, she was glittered with classy white gold and diamond jewellery, contrasting against her skin. She smiled a big, wide, warm smile as she stepped towards Sally, who thought she knew who this was, but still had a degree of caution, concerned that it was someone sent by Delroy. The new arrival to the house spoke.

"Sally, I am pleased to meet you at last, Em has told me so much about you. I really hope that we can become good friends."

Sophie turned to kiss Emily, as she placed her mobile phone and bag down on the worktop. Sally was relieved and casually continued to prepare the dinner as she greeted Sophie. Not letting on how concerned she had been to her sister, appearing to remain calm and as cool as the rest of the family did, in any potential situation. She understood the attraction between her little sister and her girlfriend. The calm, classy, attractive lady, stood before her oozing friendliness and an upbeat liveliness, which was combined with a sense of humour. She took an instant like to Sophie, realising that they could easily become friends. Sally took a drink from her glass, disappointed with herself that she had been so jumpy, so concerned at someone entering the apartment, who had obviously possessed a key. She started to feel a little silly that she had been so over sensitive, considering that Emily had not shown any signs of concern and it was her apartment that was being accessed.

The three girls enjoyed their evening, finishing the meal that they had cooked. They rapidly became acquainted with each other, gaining an insight into each other's thoughts, feelings, aspirations and outlook on life. Sally gave the façade that she had started to relax, believing that all was well.

Sophie had joined them, creating a distraction for Sally, adding a new, enjoyable, purpose to the evening. She also had the knowledge from Emily, that her father had given Pete full reassurances that she was safe and well. Deep down however, this was far from the case. She wondered if Pete had received his instructions from her father, was he heading out to France on the classic car run and was Delroy still around. She struggled to act out the relaxed, happy person that she was insisting on portraying, although Sophie's personality was greatly assisting her to play the role. Contained within her soul was the desire to do something. She believed she should be doing something active, hopefully constructive, to ensure Pete's safety, but just how much risk of danger was she in herself?

The early hours of the morning arrived, Emily was to head out to do a small tour of the main clubs and bars, to deliver wages to the door staff, while collecting any takings. It did not involve visiting each establishment; the ones close together were already being combined by the staff. They agreed that Sophie would accompany Emily to minimise any risk due to the current situation. Sally was happy to be left on her own for a few moments. Pleased to have her own space for a short time. The apartment was located in the town centre, so close to all of the nightlife venues; the total trip was to be only a few minutes.

The girls left, Sally was alone for a while, enjoying those few precious moments to herself. She started to feel upset, Pete may be at risk and that she was a prisoner in the apartment. It may be a luxurious penthouse with her sister and her partner, but she still felt restrained, frustrated that there was the world out there, beneath the sky, moon and stars. That this was something that she had to remain isolated from. She felt helpless at the situation and that she was not in control. As a lawyer she was used to having a degree of control, to be in a position of authority in a crisis, not being expected to sit back and be controlled, allowing something to happen to her. The one consolation was that she knew Alice would be safe. The advantage of Alice's autism being that she was never left unattended, she needed the constant support of an adult. There was no opportunity for her to be approached and influenced by anyone else. She was happy that the school was secure, with locked gates and constant supervision. The journey to and from the school by the taxi and escort, also did not present any risk. At home Antonie would be there, taking good care of her, in the protected, secure, walled environment of their home.

Emily and Sophie returned to the apartment, placing the takings from sales by the door staff onto the dining table for counting, prior to its being concealed. It was of course all cash, something that had great advantages, but did have the disadvantage that concealment was required.

"Sally, Sally we are back. Let's get the chocolates out with the spirits. We have nothing on tomorrow, so let's make this a good night. But no embarrassing stories about when I was a child, not in front of Sophie."

Emily's suggestion was falling on deaf ears, no reply was heard. They both checked out all of the rooms in the apartment, thinking that Sally must have been in the bathroom, or bedroom. There was no one present. The apartment was empty. Sally had gone.

There was no note, no indication as to whether she was safe. Had Delroy found out her location and abducted her? Had she foolishly gone into town to absorb some night air? Or had she left, to head for home, or to try to find Pete? The girls both experienced mixed emotions, being both worried and annoyed. Annoyed that she may have foolishly left, especially without telling them, but concerned that she may have been removed against her will. Even if she had left the apartment voluntarily, under her own steam, it did not mean that she was safe. She was likely to be out there alone, with no protection, no one aware of her location. The girls decided to split. Emily driving around to try to locate her, asking questions of the most trusted door staff, although they were now mostly heading home, while Sophie remained at the apartment praying for her to return.

All enquiries struck a blank, although only limited approaches could be made. It was not possible to go too far into investigating the likely whereabouts of someone who was already missing. A missing person cannot be more missing, than they already are. Contacts would be already looking out for her, both around the region and further afield.

Cautious of using the telephone, Emily drove up the hill to her father's drive. He was fully aware of the deal and she had come clean with him as to what was going off. She realised that in the current situation, he needed to know about Delroy, needed to know what was happening, he was the best source of protection for them all. Not just the fatherly, family, protective instinct, triggered off by any problems with his two daughters and the father of his granddaughter, but because that is the role that he carried out for a living. The role that people paid for him to carry out, both the people in the area who acted on the right and wrong side of the law used him. His business is for protection and he was very good at it, in fact he was the best. The image, his bulk, his reputation and the actions that he had carried out historically, had earned him the reputation. His status had placed him on a pedestal, people stood to defend him and his family because of whom he was. There was one area that he had not been briefed about; that of Sophie. It was something that Emily was determined to tell him, but only when the time was right.

She was adamant that this would only take place after her stupid, older sister, had come clean with Pete after all of these years. She could see how difficult that may be, how Pete may not take the news lightly and may consider that Sally has misled him for over ten years. She also believed, due to the strength of the relationship between them, that this would not create any long lasting problems. She just hoped that he could overcome any disappointment, mistrust or feeling of being deceived and find the whole situation slightly amusing. The more she thought about the situation, the worse she thought it was that her sister had divided her life in such a way, maybe getting trapped unintentionally into continuing the divide.

Emily was determined not to create the same situation with Sophie and her father. Sophie knew whom her father was alright and was fully aware of the business; in fact that was how they had first met. There had initially been a business relationship between the two of them. This had led onto the personal relationship, quickly evolving into the intimate level. What had surprised her was the velocity and intensity of her feelings, how they had dramatically multiplied beyond any control. She desperately wanted to share her happy news with her father.

She was increasingly convinced that he may accept the situation, but only after Pete became one of their family. This acceptance could only occur after his role as grandfather, was firmly and formally awarded with Alice. She knew that this was the lead that was required before her news was announced. That was something that had caused her to grow increasingly annoyed at her sister, over the last few months. If it was not for Sally, secretes she kept, her undercover lifestyle, then she would have been able to introduce Sophie from the start, to share her happy news and feelings with the father that she adored. Emily had always worshiped him, right from her first memories from childhood; she had always been determined to follow in his footsteps, progress the business as far as she could. She realised that she did not have his brute force, but also realised that the female approach could often diffuse a situation. People would often be less guarded with her than they were with her father, especially the male population. As her father grew older, he was more and more dependent upon the staff as he started to relax a little, well paid, trusted, hired help could always provide the muscle when it was needed. Much of the work involved setting people against each other rather than direct intervention, planting a few seeds and stories in the right places. This was where Emily had become an absolute master of the art.

Emily reflected on how she first learnt and practised the basic skills of setting people against each other, the manipulative skill of using others to get her own way. This was something that she had learnt back in primary school. She was also soon respected as a tough girl, having been involved in playground fights with both genders, yet still being one of the girls. She always had a protective and supportive, caring part of her nature, although mostly only exhibited to her closest friends. Her love and desire for Sophie had certainly changed her outlook on life. She had become desperate for the whole family to become fully united, truthful with each other. For now though, all of that was on hold, the pause button had to be pressed and the frames frozen, transformed into nothing but still snapshots. They had to be animated, brought back to life with artistic craft and design at a later date. A date when Sally and Pete were out of danger and the money for the Red Diamond was firmly in her possession.

Emily was not happy with the risk that she and Sophie may get exposed in the process of locating Sally. She realised and accepted that it had to be managed in the risk matrix of life, that mitigation measures were in place, that the situation was contained within her accepted appetite for risk. If her father found out the news a little early, so be it, she had been forced into this position by Sally, so would have her to thank if all went wrong. She realised that things were now how they were, now Sally had left, or been taken from the safety of her penthouse. There had been many rumours about her over the last few years, it went with the job, and her role often involved upsetting people and some less than pleasant situations. It was all part of the day job, an occupational hazard, so if the truth about Sophie escaped, then there was a good chance that in the short-term, it would be considered nothing more than gossip, nothing that could be relied upon. The secret was something however that she was bursting to share with the world, especially her father. Emily just could not get her mind around the actions and intentions of her sister, who had divided her life for all of this time.

The CCTV system alerted her father of her arrival well before she reached his contemporary house. He had not returned to the house long ago, having been out to check on some of the security staff who were looking after construction sites, or industrial and retail premises that they guarded during the night. He joined his youngest daughter in the hallway, his bulk filling the doorway from the lounge.

"Dad, she has gone. I do not know if Delroy has found her and taken her, or if she has decided to go walkies. I went to collect the takings, I was no more than twenty minutes and she had left. I do not think she would have opened the door to anyone as there is the entry system with video. There was no sign of a struggle and I am sure she would have left some type of clue. I think she may have left to try to get to Pete."

"Fucking hell. She cannot do as she is told for a moment, even when her life depends upon it, even literally. She is so damn strong willed and full of her own intentions, never willing to take advice in a crisis as she wants to be in control, taking the lead. I agree though, knowing Sal, she will have gone to Pete. He is on his way to France this morning. I assume she will not have just happened to have her passport in her pocket, when you called her over, so she will not get too far, so will not be heading to France."

"Dad, any news on Delroy?"

"No, he has not been seen all night. Not sure what he is up to at the moment. The only person I have really spoken to today is Pete, I kept avoiding his calls, but after about the thousandth call badgering me to find out if there was any news on Sally, I answered. I give him one thing; he is certainly concerned, loves and is trying to do his best for our Sal. He said he feels helpless as he does not know her family, so cannot contact her sister to check that she is alright. I cannot reassure him now can I? I kept him in the dark so that when he contacted other people, his emotions would be genuine, straight from the heart, better than any Oscar winning performance that could be acted. Now I can hardly tell him that Sal is alright, when we have no fucking idea if she is alive or dead, off on a mission being a maverick looking for Pete, or abducted by Delroy bloody Patterson. That would be wrong, too wrong. What if it was found out that something bad had happened after we had given him reassurances that she was alright? That is playing with emotions and totally unfair. I did not give him reassurances that she was alright for a reason, for Sally's sake and I am damn sure that he will thank me for that, if I tell him why at some future point in time."

"I'm just so worried about her, I think she will have left to find Pete, but she will not, if he is about to enter France."

"Sal is no fool, never has been, never will be. She will have no passport with her and I cannot see her heading for home for it, she would consider it too risky. She may head for a port, or the Channel Tunnel, looking out for a convoy of old cars, but my money is on Jersey. From what you have told her, she knows that Pete is heading there, after calling at France only briefly. They both love the island and have visited there on many an occasion. She will head out to Jersey without a doubt. On arrival she will be faced with two choices, I am not sure which she will opt for. It will either be hang around the airport anticipating his arrival from France, or head out to some special place of theirs, some bay that they love. After all, the first thing Pete will do after dropping off his baggage will be to visit some place that is special to the pair of them, especially if we remain silent and do not pass any details to him."

The father and youngest daughter discussed the options, wondering what could be done, if anything to ensure Sally's safety. They decided that trying to find Sally themselves would be a mistake for now, they knew where she would be heading, having no doubt in their mind where her priorities would lie. Actively trying to follow her was considered, but dismissed as a grave mistake. Delroy or his associates may be monitoring them, trying to approach Sally would achieve nothing, apart from leading the predator to its desired pray. The focus for the staff, the ears on the street and within the police force must therefore have one objective in mind; locating and following the movements of Delroy. If he headed in the direction of Pete and potentially Sally, they could intervene, if he did not, at least it offered some degree of comfort that their sister and daughter would be safe. Meanwhile someone on the payroll, someone less obvious, someone with an association not well known, could head to Jersey, to be on site if any action materialised. For now they dismissed that Delroy would have tried anything close to home. They anticipated that he would consider that the risks would be too great. The knowledge in the area that Sally was missing was too high, too many people, in too many places, were looking out for her.

***

What Sally had not been prepared to do any longer, was to sit back, waiting for the situation to be resolved by others. She had gathered a few belongings, including her driving license that was in her handbag and left. The comfortable and safe apartment faded into the distance, as she had ventured out into the night. There were few people around as she got a taxi from the town centre. It was strategically located, waiting to entice the drunken stragglers, who were vacating the clubs. Her destination was the airport.

She wanted to get to France, to meet Pete across the Channel, but obviously had no means of making the trip without her passport. Heading back to the house, with the risk of being noticed by Antonie, or anyone else, was too great a risk. Even with the passport, a journey into another country would have involved a level of risk. Someone who was supposed to be missing may have been identified when yielding a passport, attempting to leave the country. Jersey it was to be, she prepared herself to wait a few hours for the next flight. She was frustrated that she could not use her mobile, but the hacking risk was too great. She wanted to tell Pete what she was doing, that she was coming over to meet him, realising that they may get to Jersey at a similar time, although from opposite directions across The Channel.

If all of the timescales had gone to plan, as per the information that Emily had provided, Pete should be on his way to France now. He would be driving down to the channel tunnel, or ferry, depending upon which route his fellow club members had chosen to take. She was well aware that Pete would have intended to breakdown in France as early as possible, before heading out to Jersey. That way the car could be quickly and easily recovered, dispatched home along with its cargo. Acting quickly reduced risk and added to the efficiency of the operation. She knew all she had to do was to get to Jersey unnoticed and wait.

Chapter 13

Making Enemies

Delroy Patterson was not a happy person. He was far from it, he liked to pride himself in his tough guy, muscular image, something that he attempted to model on his idol; Mark Daniels. The only problem was, in comparison he was nothing, never was and never would be. He lacked the aura that surrounded Mark, the image and the power. He was nothing more than an attractive man of Jamaican decent, with a great toned, muscular body. He never realised that the power held by Mark, was not something that could be purchased. There was no quick fix to win the respect of the criminal gangs, individuals, plus the law abiding citizens of the region. This was something that would just never happen, the region would never be his, and the respect would never be forthcoming. He was confused. How in the line of work that they operated in, could a girl inherit the power and the status? Why was she being placed on the pedestal, without having the bulk and muscle of a typical hard guy? Del was strong, muscular, well-toned and physically fit. The advantage that he had over many of the people, whom he came into literal contact with, was his speed. He was agile, with an edge that many of the larger, more bulky men in the industry, just did not have.

His attributes were however, a great asset in other areas of his life. He was on the face of it a nice chap, confident and with a physical appearance that gained attention. He was popular with the girls and ladies, very popular, but he knew it. He used his looks with great success, having a number of conquests. A week did not pass by, without Delroy having a beautiful woman for company. He usually had his pick from several girls, selecting the one whom he preferred. He was never in the position of ever having to compromise, spending time with anyone that just happened to be on offer, when he fancied a night of female company. He had developed an eye for the ladies and a bit of a reputation, but his appearance still worked, adding to his success in this area of his life. This had developed his ego; it had expanded out of all proportion, gaining a slightly cocky edge to his personality.

From time to time he found someone who meant more to him, a girl which he wanted to spend more than the occasional night with. They had something more special to offer, either in terms of personality, looks, or the ability to provide him with a higher level of sexual satisfaction. Emily had fallen into this longer term category and he genuinely had feelings for her, it was more than a combination of the above factors. She was accompanied by an additional dynamic, a dimension that only she could offer; power and image. She was the boss's daughter, not any old boss who was a mere source of employment and income, but the person who possessed the ultimate tough guy image, respected by all parts of society, who controlled the region. Not only this, but the girl on his arm also had the same image, the same power, force and respect had been inherited by her, despite being of the fairer sex.

These were addictive ingredients for Delroy, the ultimate goal, bringing him an attractive female companion with its associated trimmings, while creating an image, which in his mind at least, was second to none. He anticipated the levels of respect that would follow, from both the criminal and law abiding community, all through his relationship. Not only that, he did like her, Emily had the package of attributes that he looked for in a girl, without the added ultimate bonus, he would have still welcomed her to his bed. Maybe not for so long and not with the intensity that had developed in this relationship, but they were still there.

He received the respect from the law abiding community, they now saw him as now being one of the Daniels. To be fair, it also offered a significant degree of success with the petty thief, those that ranked at the lower end of the crime spectrum. Where it went wrong, which was outside of his understanding, was that the accolade of the higher ranking criminal fraternity, was simply not forthcoming. They took no notice of him whatsoever. He did not expect to develop the power of Mark; he was on a pedestal, in a league of his own, a hero, a god to be worshiped by all. His disappointment was that none of it rubbed off on him, not where the people who really mattered were concerned. They had the respect for Emily, which was genuine; she was placed on the red carpet wherever she went. No matter what situation she was in, she had become an A-listed celebrity throughout the underworld, clearly inheriting her father's attributes. As for himself however, he was not being considered any differently from before, just viewed as someone who worked for them. This confused and irritated Delroy; he was with her much of the time and shared the intimate moments within her, in her bed.

His financial reward was also not really any better, he was paid, received a salary and nothing else. Emily treated him to clothes and items that he wanted, but that was all. The family seemed rich, having plenty of money and a continual high income from somewhere that was never revealed.

The only thing he did gain from them; was some degree of insight. He had a greater awareness of what was happening on the street, either from the family, or gained from others. Mark in particular, had started to trust him. Delroy hoped it was a form of acceptance to the family, almost a precursor of becoming a potential son-in-law. It was not so much that business matters were shared with him, even in part, yet alone in full. He had never reached those dizzy heights; it was more that conversations between Mark, Emily and Andy – an aging bodybuilder, who had been working for Mark from his first beginnings – were less guarded around him. They would mention small amounts about deals and happenings in front of him, something that they had never done before.

Mark had tended to often be the person who initiated such discussions, so Delroy was aware of the increased level of trust that he was being rewarded with. He had now gained small, but meaningful data on activities, especially around the import of packages from mainland Europe, and the market for jewels over in Jersey. What he had never managed, was to piece together the full picture from the various sound bites. He never gained enough knowledge to assemble a complete story. That was something that annoyed him, like watching a film intermittently, not ever becoming familiar with the plot, what the story was truly about. This resulted in more than an element of confusion.

Over the last few months, his ego had been damaged and his confidence knocked. He had become physically and mentally hurt, by two separate incidents. The emotions turned from pain and disappointment, into anger. An anger that was starting to put pressure on his brain, until it started to hurt behind his eyes. The anger grew, multiplying, growing in intensity until he became restless and frustrated. He felt that he was to explode. It would just be a matter of time before the anger took over, encapsulating his whole being, leading him to undertake an activity fuelled by anger, rather than by thought. What he was yet to realise, was the magnitude and the severity of the impact on his life, these two events were to have.

A couple of weeks after starting to go out with Emily, Delroy was on a high. He had decided that he had made it, that he was now in a position of power, convinced that he had been elevated into a position of respect. It had certainly worked with the lads enjoying the nightlife in town on a Friday and Saturday night, they were viewing him not only as a stud, but also as seeing Emily Daniels. He was now a testosterone-filled stallion, partly due to the activities initiated by Emily.

He now wanted to establish his image in the underworld, the true underworld, those who undertook the main criminal activity in the area and beyond. He soon decided upon his pray, the ideal candidate that he needed to convince first, so that he would be considered someone out of the same mould as Mark. He chose the person who had always treated him with contempt, often made fun of him, sometimes pushing passed him if he was standing on a door; Lee Field. Lee undertook all different types of activity, anything that would make him money, providing that it was of a reasonable scale. He liked the buying and selling of drugs in larger quantities, stately homes, jewellers, anything of any size. He never touched anything where he considered the reward would be too low, not worthy of the time and risk employed in achieving the result. Extortion was also a friend of his, but much of the activity was undertaken outside of the region, not in his home patch.

Delroy knew what he was up to and decided that next time he made fun of him, or pushed passed him; he was going to remind him of his manners. He was a successful criminal, who made significant financial returns and cleverly ensured that if the police were on to a job, that he was safe. It was someone else who was in the wrong place, at the wrong time, with evidence to accompany it. He however, was comfortably sitting back, in the company of the perfect alibi. Delroy had no problem with the way which he made his living. He did have a problem with the way that he was polite and respectful to Mark and to Andy, who was the most senior person in the business, outside of the family unit. He however, treated Delroy as a nothing, a no one and he was determined that this attitude was to change. If he changed the attitude of Lee, then the thoughts of others would be sure to follow, Lee was in a position of influence.

Lee Field was not a big guy, he appeared to have little muscular bulk, in fact, he was lean, wiry, thin, a hard man, but far from having bulk. He was of average height, average weight, build and aged in his late fifties. Delroy decided that this was the perfect match in terms of both hierarchical position and size. The next time Lee was rude, pushing passed him, he would simply put out his arm and move across to stop his entry. If Lee started on him, then he would use force to push him to the wall, restrain him, asking him to display some manners and respect, after all, he was now almost one of the family. He realised that simply challenging Lee, without hitting him, or using violence of any kind, just a degree of controlled restraint if required, would win him some respect. Respect that he felt that he now deserved. People for some reason did not challenge Lee; they allowed him to continue with his cocky, aggressive, self-centred, ignorant approach to everyone.

One night the opportunity arose. He was standing at the door of a bar; Mark was inside with Emily, probably scheming about something. It was a Friday night, so there were plenty of people around. He had been inside, but had been asked to relieve one of the door staff for a few minutes break. Heading towards him, was a small figure, in his late fifties, with blond spiky hair, moving rapidly as he always did; it was Lee. He was always rushing around; he walked quickly with purpose at all times, constantly moving around with twitchy, jerky movements. He walked up to the door, his lined, wrinkled face evident in the lights from the bar. Lee's hard, staring, steely-blue eyes were not looking at Delroy, or indeed past him, but right through him. Despite his muscle, he was totally transparent and invisible to Lee. Delroy was prepared; this was to be his ideal moment of glory, the opportunity that was building up to bring him true respect. He was clearly intending to head straight past him, expecting him to step aside. Not slowing, Lee walked to the door, Delroy stayed firm, stiffening his muscle, standing straight and strong, his determination bubbling up inside him, together with his plan. Lee spoke as he turned to Delroy.

"Shift, tosser."

He started to barge past, taking no notice of the muscle on the door. As he spoke, Delroy's rage grew; he looked straight into Lee's hard eyes and started to push him to the side.

"Did you mean; excuse me, Sir?"

In one swift moment, Delroy moved back to rest upon the wall, as Lee walked straight through. Delroy clutched his stomach, feeling that he had been hit, although he had no recollection of Lee actually doing anything. The dull thud he felt in the stomach, turned to a more intense pain, his hand felt wet as he looked down, he saw red. Blood was seeping through his fingers.

Lee walked quickly and purposely into the bar, approaching Mark and Emily.

"Evening you two, how are you doing?"

"Yes we are fine, thanks Lee, how about yourself?"

"Better than that silly little boy that you have put on the door, looks like some youth has cut him with his penknife for a laugh. Society, what is it coming to? The youth probably had to save two weeks pocket money to buy the blade to do that. If he had anything about him, he would have done a proper job, steeling something worth having in the process."

Sophie went to the door; Delroy was leaning on the wall, trying to hide what had happened, still clutching his stomach. A small amount of blood gradually soaking through his shirt, he slowly slid down the wall and slumped to the floor.

The crowd surrounded him, not one of the customers who were enjoying their night out had noticed a thing, the action being so fast, so slick. Everyone thought Lee had simply walked passed him, even Delroy did not realise what had happened until it was over. A night in hospital and he was back on his feet, although his confidence had been battered, some of the cockiness had faded. He knew to keep his mouth shut. That he had made a stupid move to try to tame Lee Field. If he came clean, Emily and Mark would say that he got what he deserved. He was starting to learn, achieving the power and status amongst the street youngsters was easy, and influence was simple. This could be achieved by association, whom one was connected to and friendly with. When it came to the real, true, underworld, that was a different matter completely, the image and associations stood for nothing, absolutely nothing. The world that he wanted respect from was a little tougher than he had believed. The one thing he did believe; was that Lee would keep it quiet, not telling Mark what he had done. To Lee this was nothing, he had done nothing, to him this stabbing was as simple as asking someone to stand aside, of total insignificance, forgotten within the moment. If Mark had found out, it is Delroy whom he would be angry with, one of the first rules of the business was not to pick on your own, not without good reason. Not to act against those under the umbrella of protection.

There was one thing that concerned him, the failed plan for respect did not matter, that was fading into insignificance, he now realised that he could wait his turn to gain respect. It did not matter for now that this incident had, if anything, halted his progress, been an interruption to his planned career and image. The problem was more deep seated, more dangerous. He realised that this had just been a little warning, a superficial flesh wound. His card was now marked. He had received his first warning from Lee, that next time if he crossed his path, he would not be so lucky. Delroy knew that to his dying day, he would remember the night and hate Lee. He would file the incident away, make nothing of it, but it would be stored, to be brought forward at a future point if needed. The problem was, he also knew the feeling would be mutual, Lee would not forget the challenge either.

Delroy still had an eye for the ladies, although he had managed for once, to be completely faithful to Emily. This was not just through his choice and his feelings for her, although to be fair, they were growing to a level that they did not usually reach. He realised that without her, he was nothing, and if he got caught he would have Mark to answer to. Keeping his tackle strictly only engaged with one girl was something new to him, but something that he knew he had to do, otherwise there was every probability that Mark would find out and remove it totally, without aesthetic. In fact, Mark had basically told him that, back when they first started seeing each other. Although Mark was smiling at the time, making light of it, he somehow doubted that it was indeed in jest at all. That it was a threat, and Mark's reputation stated that the threat would not be an idle one. He kept his eyes strongly focused on Emily, well, at least, when anyone was around. What mattered was that he did not act on any thought.

There was one girl who did distract him slightly, one that he came across more and more frequently. She was tall, dark, of mixed race, beautiful and had a confident way with her, one that exuded class and style. He did not have to go far to see her, or indeed, risk getting caught by Emily, as she was usually in her penthouse. Her new best friend; Sophie was becoming a frequent visitor and a regular subject of girls' nights out, or girls' nights in. These were both concepts beyond Delroy's comprehension. After all, why would she not want to spend all of her time with him?

He would have become jealous of their friendship, the amount of time that they were spending together and the private jokes that they regularly shared. One thing prevented all of this; her looks. He was perfectly happy to have someone so aesthetically pleasing, visiting the same apartment as him. He could sit back, with a drink in hand and turn to look at Emily, or at Sophie, taking in the view, liking what he saw. In addition there was no risk of him getting into trouble for it. She was Emily's friend, invited in, so he was obliged to be friendly with her. All he wanted now was for them both to climb into bed with him at the same time, although he doubted that this would ever happen, it was something that he could imagine. The thoughts had been distant, until one night when Sophie was staying in the spare room, the two girls kissed each other goodnight. The only thing that was wrong was that Emily was becoming a little more distant from him, this combined with a little hostility from Sophie, reduced his enjoyment of the experience.

He had made enquiries with his fellow staff in the business, trying to establish if Emily had been spotted with any other man, after all, they provided the security at all of the local clubs and bars. All reports had come back with a clean bill of health. The only person she had been seen with, apart from various business related meetings with different people, which were clearly identified as what they were, was Sophie. That at least put his mind at ease. Sophie despite her looks had never been seen with a man. He was happy that she was not the type of girl who would be seeing several people, encouraging Emily to do the same. He reached his own conclusion of what had happened; that Lee had gone and spilt the beans, letting out the truth of how he had become stabbed. Delroy concluded that in his daily analysis of the incident, it had resulted in leaving him looking naive and weak. This had angered Delroy, the anger was gradually swelling up inside him, along with increasing frustrations, and he was now on edge. He was not just annoyed with Lee, but at himself, the situation, and with everyone who was not giving him the respect that Emily and Mark received.

Delroy received some news that pleased him; Lee Field had been taken into questioning by the police. He had allegedly pulled off a raid of cash and a collection of jewellery from a stately home, somewhere in Hampshire where Sophie originated from. The news soon spread around that it had been a big deal, that there was a girl involved who had caused a distraction while the robbery took place. This was great news for Delroy, he could not be happier that Lee may end up serving time, that he may be sent away on a government paid holiday for a few years. It would give time for people to forget what had happened, allowing him to improve his image within the sector of society that he was so desperate to impress. He laid frantic plans to become involved in the 'in crowd'. With Lee out of the way, this would be the perfect opportunity to nestle in, deciding this time to take a softer, more helpful approach, rather than a challenge. There was one thing that could stand in the way of his plans; that Lee walked free from the Court Room, cleared and not convicted. He had heard that the evidence was against him, but the solicitor taking the brief was the usual one who tended to represent the local mafia. To date, she had an excellent track record of either her clients going free, or getting away lightly, with only short sentences being imposed. This was another beautiful young lady, although too small for Delroy's taste, she was also a frequent visitor at the apartment, a certain person named Sally, who just happened to be Mark's other daughter.

He had no time for her at the best of times. He thought Sally had a rather controlling, superior attitude towards him, with a slightly severe, almost hostile manner. Every time they met, she was always inclined to respond to him with some smart answer. She always portrayed edginess, something that he felt allergic to. Then again, that was probably why she had the success that she did in her job. He just hoped that all would fall in his favour. What he did not realise, was that all was to fall against him, he was soon to become in his eyes, the outcast from both the family and the business.

Delroy arrived at Emily's apartment in his usual cocky way. His manner had rapidly re-grown; being reborn and refuelled now that Lee had been detained. He was sure that Lee would go down, that the police would have something on him, evidence that even Sally would not enable him to wiggle his way out of. Emily had just returned from a business trip to London, followed by a few days in Jersey. Despite the fact that she had only just arrived from the airport, Sophie was already there, they were both still wearing outdoor clothes. Delroy detected something between them, not the hostility of the moments following an argument, or a minor disagreement, but something all the same, possibly a secret that they were hiding. He had become increasingly jealous of that girl, especially the time that Emily spent with her. Over the last few months, she had clearly become more interested in spending time with her, than with him. He was starting to wonder if those two were scheming and plotting something, something that he was excluded from, feeling isolated and alienated. Sophie left, after whispering something to Emily.

He was pleased that she had gone, the novelty of having another attractive woman in the apartment almost every time that he saw Emily, had gradually worn wafer thin. In fact, despite her looks and his initial thoughts of having them both in his bed together, he was becoming sick of the sight of her. She was always classily dolled up, never a hair out of place. Miss perfect, she who could do no wrong, was starting to grate on him. He wished that they would have a little bitchy disagreement over something, so that some new girl could be introduced. Maybe she would be attractive and want to start a threesome, now that his dreams of this one had gone a little sour? His feelings for Emily had not diminished, especially the desire of power. If anything, it had been amplified as he had more to do with his super hero; Mark.

"Thank fuck for that. The fashion icon has gone. What the hell does she do apart from wander around with you all day? Can't you tell her to piss off and leave us alone for a while? I can never get near you for her. Every time that I come around so that we can get together, babe, she is here. I try to give you a snog and she sits between us."

Delroy turned to place his large, strong hand firmly between Emily's legs and turned to face her, moving his other hand towards her chest. Emily turned and glared at him, then quickly stood up. Delroy was not happy, he was feeling demanding and annoyed.

"What is it now? I want a fuck."

"The only thing you can do, Del, is to fuck off! You do not approach me like that, or tell me what to do with my friend."

Delroy's temper was growing. He paced erratically around the room, his arms swinging, his dark brown eyes drilling into Emily.

"You have got someone. You bitch! You are seeing someone aren't yer? That is why you always have your lapdog with you for cover."

"If you must know, Del, yes I am. It is over."

"Who? I want to know who the fuck he is? Does he know whom he is dealing with and upsetting here? I'll cut his dick off by the time the day is out. That is whom you have been away with isn't it?"

"Yes, Del, it is, but on business. Let us get something straight here, a little correction is needed. You are nothing, a simple nobody. It is me and my father who have the power. It is you, who have forgotten whom you are dealing with here. One wrong move and you will find yourself in the river, floating towards the sea. There will be no police investigation, as there will be witnesses, good, reliable witnesses. In fact, they may even work in the police force. They would see you so high on drugs, that you decided that you could fly. They would see you on the bridge, as you shouted; *'Flight nine-one-eight coming in to land.'* They would see you hold out your arms stretched straight, preparing for your final flight. They would watch, helplessly, as you took off from Trent Bridge, landing in the fast flowing water with strong undercurrents below. It can be arranged to happen, it will not be the first time. The detail will all work. The reliable witnesses will come forward, complete with a fully corroborated story."

Delroy was getting upset. The utmost emotion however, was anger, anger at Emily, anger at whoever she was seeing. The frustration bubbled and boiled up inside him, the steam struggling to escape, building the pressure inside the vessel of his head and body. He knew there could not be a release of the steam. He could not afford to let it go, he realised deep down, just whom he was dealing with. Anything that happened would come to rest, firmly back on his shoulders. He was dealing with the Daniels here, and Emily was a force not to be crossed, he knew that. As for her father, any wrong move would indeed see him floating down stream, or worse.

Emily was playing it cool, calmly looking at him directly in the eyes, her hardness showing through. She spoke calmly, slowly, but firmly. He realised it was over, his whole plans for his image had simultaneously been switched off, in one quick action. Emily did not make idle threats, if she said something she could, and would, make it happen. There would be no danger of anything ever being pinned back on her. His demise would be an accident, having simply taken a few too many recreational drugs, when trying to cheer up after being dumped.

Delroy turned, looked at her and grinned, an unhappy grin of defeat. He shook his head and turned silently to the door. Knowing, as always, that Emily had got the better of him.

"Oh, Del, one more little thing before you go. You will not cut my new partners dick off, as she does not have one. I got used to sex without one over the months with you."

Delroy left, it was the first time he had been dumped, that was usually the task reserved only for him. Something he had done, time and time again over the years, it had always been him that had been heartless. He had often used girls for his pleasure, before moving to try the next free sample. This time it was the reverse, not only had he lost Emily, but also his image and maybe his job. To add to it all, he had been dumped for a girl. He had never considered how others had felt, now he was the one experiencing the pain.

He went to a bar to drown his sorrows, not one that either he, or the people he mixed with usually frequented. He was not in the mood to be seen, not wanting to be questioned. He wanted to think, in a location where his image did not have to be maintained. He ordered a drink and turned as he felt someone standing close to the side of him. A lean, older man, with short, spiky, blond hair and hard steely blue eyes, stood leaning on the bar. Patting him on the shoulder with a grin, he uttered the words.

"Good girl that Sally!"

He then walked off, leaving Delroy at the bar. His day could not have been worse. No Emily, no image, no power and now Lee Field freed from court, all due to the work of Mark's other daughter. He started to plan, he did not know what, but plot against those two sisters he did.

Chapter 14

Arrivals in Jersey

Sally arrived in Jersey and waited around the airport. She had felt guilty about sneaking out of the apartment, leaving her sister and Sophie without any warning, or explanation. She was too concerned to hang around, too frustrated with the situation to simply wait, sitting around all day, hoping that all would work out how her sister intended. She was worried for Pete and knew that she could not call him, deciding instead it should be safe to meet him at arrivals in the airport. She watched the screens in the airport, hoping that the timing had all gone to plan, hoping that Pete would land on the next plane from France.

A flight from Paris landed; it was the one that she hoped he would be on and watched out for the influx of travellers through arrivals. She was nervous; her heart was beating faster and pounding within her chest. To Sally, it was as if they had been separated for months, not a little over three days. Her feelings of nervousness reminded her of when they first went out together, not that they exactly met each other on dates; they just took the plunge, spending time together from the start. The stream of people flowed through arrivals with any luggage that they had, the later stragglers trickled into the airport, but no Pete. Her heart sank, she felt disappointed, lonely, abandoned, jilted, stood-up, despite the fact that Pete would have no idea she was to be there. She hoped that he had been delayed, but to no avail, he did not show. Airport staff and security were looking at her suspiciously, so she headed out into the shopping mall of the airport, she sat down, strategically locating herself to view anyone and everyone who was to leave.

She found the people watching interesting; it was something that she had a talent for; her years following university as a Solicitor had been spent looking at people across a desk. Talking to the police and those who were accused of, or had indeed undertaken a criminal act involved people watching, analysing those in front of her. All had their own story to tell, not just in words, but in mannerisms, actions, body language and through the feelings she got from people. She had a power to be able to identify the truth, to twist the truth, emphasis the truth, convince people of the truth, or of what had been decided to become the truth.

Something did not ring true with her sister's story, there was something missing, some involvement not declared. Emily was the type of person to take everything within her stride, to not overreact, but to remain calm and surefooted, even in a dangerous, or potentially violent situation. Sally realised that there was something far deeper, more sinister, a turbulent undercurrent that was being concealed. If everything had been as simple as she had said, all this concern over contact with Pete and her own location would not have existed. The whole situation would usually have been looked upon by Emily as a still millpond, calm, controlled, without any waves. She guessed it was around the Red Diamond, deciding that it was likely to be hot, having been removed without its owner's consent. What was more, her partner was about to transport it across the island. She had no doubt that this was not a cheap purchase from a banker who had hit trouble in the recession, that it would have been removed, either in its recent history, or in the past, being concealed from circulation. One element she did believe, that it was indeed being sold by Emily for several times its purchase price, but then again, even the sum of one pound, may be more than it was acquired for if her theory was correct.

Sally checked into her hotel; The Merton in St Saviour, big enough for her to blend into the background, not wanting to be the focus of any attention. It was busy due to the summer months, the attraction of the water complex for families and the good food. To Sally it was the location that mattered, it was just a pretty walk across Howard Davis Park form St Helier. Close to the hub of the island, but also an easy beach walk to where she always stayed with Pete, in a basic, rented fisherman's cottage on the La Grande Route Des Sablons at the edge of La Rocque, with direct access to the sea. She suspected that this was where Pete may have booked in if he had been able, so she would have a good chance of finding him. If it had been already booked, he would have been likely to find an alternative close by.

They had shared special, tender, intimate moments on the beach, overlooking the Seymour Tower out at sea and in the little cottage. That is where she decided to head, where she would be sure to find Pete at the cottage, or looking out to sea, waiting for news of her to arrive.

She walked purposely up the steps from the beach and hammered on the cottage door, peering through the lounge window for sight of belongings, either those of Pete, or someone else who had rented the accommodation. There was no reply; the cottage looked empty, only the sparse furnishings were evident through the small panes of glass.

It was a special place for them both, but this time she was alone, she placed herself down on a rock and looked out into the water. She thought back to first meeting Pete, what she had felt for him the second that they met. In addition to the instant attraction and love, he radiated something for her that she knew would last forever. She initially was concerned at his naivety and nervousness. For someone who was involved with property deals, he surprisingly had limited understanding of the wider outside world, or at least, the world she had been born into. From the start, she realised however that he was trainable, could be led in the direction that she wanted, to enable him to become part of her world, manipulated into her way of life.

Although he already knew her father, she made the decision to keep the two parts of her life separate. Deciding that it would be too much for him, to introduce herself as a fellow professional, then to the position she held in the underworld family. It was something that she thought needed to be merged gradually, edging the full extent of her life out, so that it joined the full flow of traffic when the time was right. This way he would understand and not dismiss some of the activity her father and sister undertook, accepting the people who were more than clients to her. She was concerned that it would have slowed things down, restricting the torrent of passion, something she did not want to happen. She wanted him at full velocity, no matter what the cost, even if that meant a little deception, or being somewhat economical with the truth. He is an understanding person by his nature, kind to her, so never pushed her on any subject that she was remaining quiet on. He always waited for her to initiate any sensitive subject, which she would raise when she was ready.

Sally had been too busy enjoying herself with Pete to bother about the intersection with her family, never getting as far as integrating them together. This was an action she was now regretting, feeling guilty of exercising her right to silence; almost misleading Pete into thinking there was something wrong with her childhood, when there was not. She had simply not found the right moment, which had become harder to search for as time had passed. She realised that she was wrong, that she should have integrated them years ago and that Emily was right. She realised her fault, how that she had made things harder for Pete to accept, increased the level of risk, all due to the passage of time. If she had integrated them from the start, she would not be here now, missing him, frantically distraught that he may be in trouble. Her tough guy father had not helped. He was so upset, concerned about his feelings when he found out that Alice was autistic. He was scared of disability, scared of weakness, not in others, he preyed on that, but where it came to himself and his family. It was not that he did not love his granddaughter, in fact quite the reverse; he was just scared of his feelings for her, further reducing the opportunities to achieve the integration.

She prayed that Pete would forgive her when she explained, that was something she was going to do just as soon as she found him. She was to take the risk and plunge right in, despite the situation. Providing they both left the island safe and well, they would be integrated and be introduced to who was whom. If they ended up on different flights back, so be it, but it had to be done. She expected some degree of fall out and pain for what she had done, she desired it, was looking forward to it, she wanted to receive the punishment and sentence that she deserved for the near betrayal. She was sure that their deep feelings for each other and what they had would overcome it, healing anything in time, of that she was certain.

When they met, she knew he was innocent. She was there, ready and waiting for the explosion, ready to capture him when he was rounded up, herded like a sheep away from the scene in her direction. The two large men that were giving chase, where Andy; her father's right-hand man and one of the other staff. Capture him she did. She had no intention of letting him go from the first time she looked into his eyes, witnessing the look in his, as he set eyes upon her for the first time. He was to be captured for life, by the power she had over him, through nothing more than true feelings. No matter what the cost, there was no way that she would ever let him part; although she was sure that he never would anyway. She was eternally grateful that the company that Pete had worked for had not treated him fairly, failing to present him with the directorship that he had deserved. She was thankful that they had rescinded on the deal for the new barn roof, upsetting her Great Uncle; Noel Harrington. Without these events, she would not have found and comprehended true love.

Her Great Uncle, was someone whom she had always liked since being a child, he always had been an eccentric character. Following the death of her mother as a child, when Emily was little more than a baby, the only member of her mother's family that had remained in contact was Noel. He was a character, and had been up to a great many activities in his younger days, although not on the same scale as her father. It was Noel and his activities, which had brought her parents together in the first place. He introduced them to each other when they were eighteen over some deal he was involved in. The then young Mark, was just starting out, aiming to construct his image. Noel had created strong love for them, which was only ended tragically by her mother's cancer. She knew her parents would have made it, remained together, if her mother had not been rudely stolen from them at a young age.

Sally had been close to her mother, always admiring her, she was the inspiration that made her decide from an early age to follow in her footsteps; into law. For Emily, she had always had the inseparable bond and admiration for her father, something that Sally was slightly jealous of. Why should her younger sister be allowed to continue with her bond, inspiration and closeness to her father, when the closeness and similarity she shared with her mother, had been forcefully disconnected at a young age? Neither her, nor her father had ever accepted her mother's death. Her Dad was in control, control of everything that occurred in his world, he had the power to change, to manipulate and influence people, behaviours, situations but not cancer. Cancer could not be controlled by a loved one, not even a tough, bulk of muscle working in the security industry.

Her mother's family, apart from her uncle Noel, had all blamed her father. They were very religious and they felt that Mark was to blame. His image, way of life, behaviours, how he made his money, were all in their eyes; wrong. So was her mother by marrying into his world. Her actions were, and still are to them, considered a great sin, that the cancer was there to take her mother back to her maker, rescue her from sin, while torturing those left behind, letting them experience hell before their death. They had all disowned her mother as soon as she moved in with Mark, Noel was already an outcast of the family, for well, just being Noel.

Sally was close to Noel, even before he introduced her to Pete. She would be eternally grateful for his character and that he had decided to bomb Pete's office. This action to him, was a perfectly reasonable behaviour, in the circumstances of being let down. The whole event was set up by Noel and her father, staged to ensure that the company that Pete had worked for received a little fright. They decided that they were doing Pete a favour, liberating him, letting him escape from the company that had not recognised his talent. Mark knew that he had clients who would provide work for Pete; he would be considered an asset and paid what he deserved.

There was never any danger to his safety, little Josh was briefed to run, to race Pete as soon as they left the car following delivery of the envelope. Making the phone call from the safety of the games store was the signal to trigger. Detective Sergeant Armstrong was also briefed to be on the scene, to be involved in the arrest, ensuring that his innocence was recognised and the story with Sally corroborated. Noel just did not realise that once again, in his own strange way, he had acted as a rather unconventional cupid, changing the life of two people forever, creating Alice, the little package of fun and mischief, despite her problems.

Sally thought about the implications and inter-relationships of a simple task on others' lives, how acts of smaller magnitude than this, can design the destiny of others. Who would have believed back then, that little eight-year-old Josh Harrington would have enjoyed the fun so much that day, that now aged nineteen, after years training in the gymnasium every day to tone his body, would have gone to work for Mark?

Sally stared out to sea, watching the waves hit the rocks of the small island and the Seymour Tower in the distance. Pete was there in her dreams, but she could not help but worry why he was not yet around. She realised that something simple could have gone wrong, he was not forced to be in trouble, but she could not control her sorrow. She watched the light diminish, fading into darkness, the tower becoming a silhouette on the skyline. She looked up at the moon and the stars, randomly stippled across the darkness of the sky, wondering where Pete was, and if he too, was able to observe the jewels above his head. She thought that he was, and for a moment they were connected through feelings, being brought together under the blanket of the same sky.

She tasted the salt water infiltrating her mouth, not the spray from the waves as the tide encroached her position on the shore, but from the tears that had welled up from her dark brown eyes and were now rolling down her face, with as much velocity as the sea. She returned to the hotel during the deserted, early hours of the morning, walking along the beach back to St Saviour, abandoning the quest until sunrise.

***

I was pleased to arrive at St Helier; the attraction of the island that both Sally and I loved had not faded, although the visit was tarnished by the situation. I was not in any mood, or had any inclination to enjoy anything. In fact, I contemplated if I would ever be in a position to enjoy life again, as my feet touched the island's shore. I hoped that being away from the mainland things would be better, start to improve, hoping for positive news. I hired a car, a Ford Fiesta, clearly identified as a tourist by the red 'H' plates wore by all hire vehicles on the island. At this time of the year, they were everywhere, driving randomly around, packed with children. As I waited for the car to be prepared I found a payphone, my mobile needing to be charged. I made two calls, the first to Sally, but yet again her phone went straight to the answering service, something that I expected, but at least I got to hear the sound of her voice. This was something that reverberated through my brain over and over, it was currently the only contact that I had. While at the telephone I made a second call, this time to Antonie to check how Alice was.

"Pete she is fine, up to mischief, but then what else did you expect? Let us face it, when is she not?"

I was pleased to ascertain that she was safe and hear her German accent, a reminder of what had become normality at home.

"Antonie, if anything happens, anything slightly unusual, or suspicious, just call Mark. I do not know what is going off, but something is and he will sort out any problems."

I drove out to a rented cottage on the La Grande Route Des Sablons at thc cdgc of La Rocque, with direct access to the sea, where I had stayed with Sally on many an occasion. I pulled down the narrow gravel drive, the tyres rattling and pushing on the deep stones as I approached the door. It was a shared drive with some other cottages, but each having its own frontage to park on, along with small, but pretty cottage-style gardens. Mark had booked the cottage before I left for France, being lucky to secure my first choice of accommodation in the beginning of the summer season. I was a day late, but luckily the owner had not given up on me attending, leaving the key in the usual arranged place. It was an old, single storey terraced fisherman's cottage, probably dating from the early part of the nineteenth century. The thick rendered walls were sparklingly whitewashed, reflecting the light of the sun as is common throughout the island. There was a small, welcoming porch with pointed windows framed by black painted shutters.

This time despite the warm, sunny weather, the cottage felt cold and empty as I stepped into the lounge. The welcoming charm was muted, subdued by being alone. I placed my belongings on the red lounge carpet, looking around the old, minimalist, basic interior that was free from any design. It was usually an escape, enjoying the basic, humble building and interior to match. Usually we would have settled in, enjoyed the escape from the realities of life, enjoying a drink, plus each other's company, absorbing the peace and quiet with the only sound being the calling of the gulls above. This time it was different, the only calling in my ears was in my mind, calling me to get out of the cottage, to cross the garden and head down the steps that lead directly to the beach. The beach was quiet, almost deserted as I hurried down the private access and onto the deep, soft sand. I stood, looking out as the waves licked against the rocks at the side of me with the Seymour Tower in the distance. The cottage was located at an interesting point, where the soft sands turned into an outcrop of rocks which projected into the sea. I stood there, in this special place, absorbing the atmosphere.

I turned to look along the beach and saw a familiar figure in the distance looking towards me. My heart doubled its pace; it was Sally, talking to someone. I glanced back at the sea, not being able to believe my eyes, my face beaming, the emotions of happiness and relief welling up inside my brain. I turned to face her; she had gone, disappeared without trace. She was not there. I turned and ran up the beach, there was no one. I called out.

"Sally! SALLY! Sal..."

The only response was the calling of the gulls overhead. I realised that I must be losing my mind, I must be mad, that the situation was too much for me, that my hopes and imagination had taken over my brain, imposing projected images behind my eyes. My heart sank, I felt low and stupid as I headed back to the cottage to try to rest.

***

The following morning Sally walked back to the beach, the place that meant so much to them. She was determined to spend the whole day there, looking out for Pete, convincing herself that he would turn up. She had not eaten, had next to nothing to drink and very little sleep. She had taken nothing apart from a bottle of water to sip, not wanting to have to leave the beach for a moment, scared that if she did, she may miss seeing Pete. She also intended to revisit the cottage periodically throughout the day until she found someone in, on the off chance that Pete had managed to book it. She would either be greeted with open arms and immense joy, or to her complete disappointment by a total stranger.

As she approached the area of the beach, she spotted a figure running down the steps from the cottage and towards the rocks. Her heart started to race, feeling the immense joy and relief that she had dreamed about as her eyes focussed on Pete. She was overwhelmed and instantly called to him, but was not close enough for him to hear above the breeze and gulls, with her voice breaking with tears of delight. She started to run towards him from the distance.

"No Sally! NO SALLY STOP!"

The familiar male voice was close by her. She turned shocked and surprised to see the red, weathered face, of Detective Sergeant Armstrong at the side of her.

"Sally, sorry. Really sorry. We must go now, quickly, before he spots us. He will be in danger if you two are found together, someone is after you."

"Armstrong, it can wait, I just need to see him."

Armstrong pulled Sally around and pushed her behind the small wall that formed the properties defence from the sea.

"Sally you must not. Trust me, you will see him soon. Come with me, I will explain, keep you safe and away from the person who is after the pair of you."

"Delroy. I know it is Del."

Sally realised that Armstrong would be right, she was upset, but all that mattered was that Pete was safe. She was pleased with the fine timing, that Armstrong had saved Pete from her own selfish intentions that could have placed them both at risk. She understood from what Emily had said that they could be at risk if they were together, being two targets in one shot.

They headed through St Helier to St Aubin in Armstrong's hired car. He was telling Sally how she was at risk, how that he had been sent over by her father to offer protection from Delroy, following her involvement in freeing Lee Field. They chatted and Sally expressed her concerns, confiding in him that Emily had tried to keep her at her penthouse, but she had come over to find Pete. They entered the edge of the pretty village of St Aubin, Armstrong leading her to a small boathouse building with windows indicating that there was a floor above. It stood close to the harbour in disrepair, contrasting with its smart surroundings. It was constructed out of a combination of stone and timber cladding on the upper parts. There were tourists around the sea front and shops, many gathered around the popular café.

"I have rented a flat above the boathouse; we can talk there, where there is no one around. Then I will drop you off back at your hotel, where you must stay put. Emily was right keeping out of sight is the safest thing to do. I have it all under control."

Opening a small door set in the corner of the large doors wide enough to facilitate the entry of a boat, they both entered the building. It was dark and cool inside, the floor laid with old cobble stones that were uneven. The lofty space with high ceiling was bare and empty apart from one item. Out of the darkness stood an old caravan with a dim light inside. Armstrong closed the door, behind them. Sally started to shiver; an element of concern was shooting through her body, together with disbelief that the long standing detective, who had been on her father's payroll for years, had brought her there rather than to a hotel. When entering the building she had assumed that the ground floor would be converted into a garage, with nice stairs leading to the apartment above. Instead the access to the upper floor was an old wooden set of open tread steps, steep and little better than a ladder. She knew that she was in trouble and could not believe what she had let happen. It was not only Armstrong's action that she was disappointed in, but her own naivety and trust in him.

A deep voice came from behind her.

"Mistake, you fucking bitch. Big mistake. Getting Lee off was a big mistake, as was your sister dumping me for that tart. I have plans for you, just you wait and see. You will regret what you did for Lee."

Sally turned to face the tall, dark, toned figure of Delroy Patterson standing staring at her. He walked towards her, placed one hand out to feel her breasts, and then raised it to hit her on the cheek.

Chapter 15

Family Protection

Mark and Emily sat in the office. They occupied the upper floor above a garage that was mainly used for the sale and repair of cars, with a focus on the cheaper, most affordable end of the market. They owned the building, letting the garage out to a trader, who in return often did them a few favours. It was a little run down, the former petrol filling station forecourt now used for car sales, with better cars kept in the small showroom and the old workshops behind. The location was ideal for their business. It was within easy walking distance into town, close to the bars and clubs that their staff spent so much time standing in front of. It had the added advantage that most town centre properties did not have; plenty of car parking. Staff and visitors could always park, door staff could park on the forecourt at night. Staff could quickly leave for a desired location if there was an alarm call, or security problem to attend to.

There was an office shared by Mark and Emily, a separate office for Andy and the administrator plus a meeting room. A large open area was made in the roof space with skylight windows, used for monitoring of any CCTV cameras, any alarm, or other surveillance activity that was being undertaken.

The offices were in need of decoration, something that despite them both being image conscious in their appearance and with their designer, contemporary homes, had never infiltrated the office. They had tatty wooden desks, quality black leather high-backed office chairs, but nothing else matched. Everything was a mismatch of acquired furniture over the years. There was little paperwork around, most either being locked away, or stored electronically away from prying eyes. They both sat facing each other while drinking coffee. Emily had her feet up on her visitor chair; her casual appearance however was betraying how she really felt within. She was worried about her sister and her partner. There had been no news from her since she had left, and there had been no sightings reported from any of her contacts. They were both assuming that they may be together in Jersey, but that was nothing more than an assumption.

"Dad, all we can do is to hope that they are together and happy, but we really do not know. I believe she will have gone to Pete, but whether they have safely found each other is another question."

"Look Em, where is the famous bloody diamond that Lee nicked from that stately home? It better be worth it, the trouble it is causing."

"Jersey. Sophie nicked it too. She deserves just as much credit for releasing it and setting it free as Lee does. Sophie is going to pose as the seller to Pete, but in actual fact, it went over there the day of the robbery, before anyone realised what was missing. It is well hidden in the cottage. We rented the same one that Sally and Pete use for a full month to give us time to move it. Sophie will just pretend to be a banker, one fallen on hard times, putting on the style and pass it over, after removing it from the hiding place."

"What are we making on the bloody diamond?"

"Red Diamond, Dad. Not sure yet, split between Lee, Sophie and us. Last time it was sold was in 1987 at an auction and it went for $880,000 that is $926,315 per carat. It is worth more now though. They are always valued in United States Dollars for some reason. Exactly how much did you tell Delroy?"

"Me, tell Del? Nothing Emily! He was around when I spoke to you about snippets of information, he could have picked that up, but that is all. I have never spoken about it in front of him. All I did was to set Pete up as courier for you as he was heading to France for me. It is you that have told him, or left something lying around. It is not my deal you should know better."

Mark was starting to get annoyed that Emily, had for once let her guard down, let the side down and let on too much about a deal. It was worth significant money, not to mention the time that Lee had almost served for its liberation, leading to Sally being put in danger. Delroy had a level of trust, but had never been accepted fully as one of the family. He was not clever enough, not able to be trusted to modify his behaviours and thoughts, to react chameleon-like to the situation that he was facing. Everything to Delroy had to be clear cut, if he was angry he showed it, there was no hidden element of surprise, no leading anyone in a different direction, he was too crude in his approach.

"No, Dad, not at all! I was drifting away from him; I found someone else whom I fell for a few months ago. He is totally in the dark and nothing is compromised. I did not do much over the phone either. I did the deal with Sophie face to face, and then the deal with the guy I am selling to, when we were over in Jersey; he wanted to see the goods. Do not accuse me of letting anything slip on this one."

They were both taken aback and were now looking out of the window and pacing around the office. Somehow Delroy had discovered too much and was to use it against Emily, Sophie, Lee, Pete and Sally. The straight talking indicating that neither of them had allowed Delroy to discover anything about the deal had come as a shock to them both. Each of them had secretly blamed each other, but neither had said anything on this subject before, they had a strong father and daughter relationship as well as being business partners. They had been prepared to let the matter go, assuming a simple error of judgement, despite the potential magnitude of the situation.

There was a knock on the door, as Lee Field paced in. The hardness of his lined face looking older than ever, he looked tired, even by Lee's standards. He was smoking a roll up, looking concerned. He joined the existing pacing around the office, choosing not to sit down. With his quick, jerky movements, always on the go, he naturally kept moving, never turning his back in any direction for too long. He was ever suspicious of who may be behind him, something that went with his success in his chosen career.

"Guys, any news on wonder Sal?"

Mark answered.

"No, not a damn thing! I suspect she is in Jersey. What about Delroy?"

"Nothing, I cannot kill the fucking scum, until I can find him. He has not been seen anywhere."

Emily looked at Lee firmly, straight into his eyes.

"Lee, I know you think I let something out to Delroy, but I did not, neither did Dad. Alright, he may have picked up the odd snippet of information, just the same as anyone else around here, but he knows nothing about the Red Diamond. If news did not spread from us, and not from you or Sophie, how the hell does he know anything? Does anyone else know from your side?"

"No one, Em. You know me; I'm a loner unless I am in on a deal with someone like Soph. No one knows anything from me. There is no word on the street, apart from what has been in the media. The only people, who were going on about the rock to me, were the police."

Mark moved around, head butted the wall, letting out a groan he threw his now empty coffee mug across the room at the wall opposite. The pottery shattered across the floor into fragments of various sizes, an indentation to the plaster marking the point of impact, an everlasting impression of his strength and the force generated by his arms.

"Armstrong. The investigation was headed by fucking Armstrong!"

Mark punched his fist against the wall, again leaving an indentation. His face was grimacing with annoyance. His temper was being demonstrated at full force, not at anyone but at himself. The others stepped back, taken aback, even Lee shocked by the magnitude of the outburst of force that he had witnessed. In addition to the physical signs, was the words themselves, the name of the Detective Sergeant who had been one of their key insiders within the force for many years. Mark was turning from red to pale, breathing slowly and forcefully, trying to control his temper enough to enlighten Emily and Lee.

"I met him last week. He leaves the force anytime, he has been given a date. He wanted a pension for life, a nice little nest egg. I told him he would be paid at his current rate for a year, plus a little retirement present, then no more. After a year out of the police, he is of no use to us. His enquiries to colleagues would cause more harm than it is worth. He was not happy about it. He has done well out of us all of these years, and a further year with a nice little bonus would be enough to get his retirement off to a good start. He has gone and got greedy on us. That is who has told Delroy, as he knows you were guilty. It is him that Delroy has joined with, not a rival from another region, just a greedy, old, bent copper, who has got too big for his station."

Lee stared across the room at Mark.

"Mark, he made contact, telling me that there are still people in the force looking at this one who think that I am guilty, telling me that I was not to move around, or to leave England as they were waiting for the Diamond to change hands, probably off shore."

Emily was turning white, as she looked at her father and at Lee.

"Armstrong? Dad, why, after how good we have been to him, would he get so greedy? He should have lined his nest for the future through us."

Both Mark and Lee looked at each other sniggering, pulling faces and raising their eyebrows at each other, not being able to accept what an obvious, naive question Emily had just asked.

"Darling, I sometimes wonder about you. We are a great team, but sometimes you cannot see what is in front of your nose, cannot hear what people do not say. Do you need glasses and a hearing aid? Why do you think Armstrong is bent? Why do you think he sits in the car listening to the sport on the radio every afternoon? Why is the Racing Post always on his back seat? Every spare penny he has is given away, donated to the bookmakers. Nothing but a looser with a habit is our Armstrong."

Lee looked at the others while shaking his head, his face was grimacing with the reality. He spoke, his voice firm, but quiet.

"Armstrong knows I intend to kill Del. It is obvious, anyone who tries it on with your beautiful girls I will take down. I owe Sal my freedom several times over. No one will survive hurting, or making her life uncomfortable while I am breathing."

Emily had caught on to the situation, desperately concerned for her sister and also trying to improve her image with Lee and her father. She realised that she had been stupid enough for the last few years to simply accept Armstrong, who had been around on the payroll since she was a child. She was kicking herself at her naivety, as to why he did what he did. She had never questioned his motives, just accepted what he did for them on face value. She realised that in this type of work that was a catastrophic mistake to make.

“It proves where he is – if Armstrong wants you to stay in England that must mean that Del is in Jersey, not wanting you to go after him as he needs him. The old detective needs his youthful muscle, anger, daring and plain stupidity.”

The phone rang, it was Andy. He spoke to Mark, telling him that Delroy’s car had been found parked at the airport, but there was no sign of Armstrong’s car. There was however, a Racing Post left in the front foot well of Delroy’s black Mercedes, something that he would not have purchased. It proved that they were together, that they had indeed joined forces and headed off to Jersey. This modified the dynamic and intensity of the meeting. The combination of the two meant that they were at risk of being exposed and that Sally could be in real danger. If she spotted Delroy she would run, hide, head for safety. She may even head for the police, explaining that she is a specialist criminal defence lawyer, with an enemy of one of her clients after her since proving his innocence in court. The Jersey Police would take the story, act giving her protection, as everything would be justifiable if they made a couple of calls to England. If it happened, they would soon be around the island looking for him, providing a solicitor with the protection that she deserved. She was not connected to anything that was not legitimate and legal.

If Sally on the other hand spotted Armstrong, she would do the inverse, head straight to him, believe him, trust him, and go where he wanted her to go by her own free will. She would believe that he was there to help her, that he was on the island to arrest Delroy, not as his accomplice.

“Dad, Lee, I will go. It is not safe for Sophie to pretend to be the vendor of the Diamond to Pete. I will be more use and Pete does not know me anyway, we have never met; only been in the same bar together. I will be on the next flight out. Delroy hates Sally and will want to hurt her. Armstrong wants the money from the Red Diamond, so will insist that Sally is unharmed until he gets his grubby little hands on the cash. Keeping the deal going buys us time, it keeps Sally safe until

Armstrong realises there is nothing in it for him. By that time it will be over, we will have Delroy and Sally."

Lee grinned.

"Protecting your darling Sophie are we? Arrhh, how sweet love is. Delroy is mine, though. Mine, remember that."

Emily turned a deep shade of crimson, mouthing the word 'bastard' to Lee. Mark as alert as ever, picked up the evidence, shook his head and sighed. The actions had done nothing apart from confirm the suspicions that he already had. He had suspected for some time that Sophie was her latest lover.

"Lee, you stay put, it is about my daughters here, and my decision about payment of Armstrong. I need a word with our Detective Sergeant friend. You can still have Delroy; I will bring him back for you. I will not spoil your fun. You take care of Sophie though. I do not want my sort of son-in-law in trouble in Jersey, then my sort of daughter-in-law in trouble over here, besides, you need to stay clear of bloody diamonds for a while. I'll take one of the lads who is a bit lighter on their feet than me, pal."

"Mark, you mean lighter full stop."

Lee was not able to resist getting a little dig in to Mark, even in the circumstances. Lee was a hard case and could not wait to get his hands on Del. Emily headed out to Jersey immediately, the muscle following on a later flight.

Chapter 16

Red Diamond

I woke up suddenly, not sure at first where I was. My first reaction was that of pleasure, I was looking around, seeing the familiar, basic bedroom of the rented cottage in Jersey, the room that was synonymous with pleasure. I then realised that I was here alone, that Sally was missing and that life had fallen apart. It then occurred to me why I had woken up, the background noise in the quiet old cottage was getting louder, it was an unfamiliar sound at first, that of someone banging on the front door. I stood, my brain becoming enlightened with the heavy load imposed within. It may be Sally? I ran to the source of the sound, almost falling over my luggage still placed on the lounge floor and excitedly opened the door.

My heart sank, returning to the murky depths that it had been at, prior to the white tongue and groove timber item being pulled open. It did not reveal the return to utopia that I had wished for. The pressure of the heavy load, was imposed on my brain once more. The figure at the door was not my dream girl, it was not Sally.

In another life I may have been pleased to see this visitor, although not of the aesthetics that I personally find pleasing, it was a pretty young lady. She was around five feet-eight, slim but of a strong build, with well-toned muscles. She appeared to be someone who was physically fit, obviously took pride in attending the gym. She was however feminine, with well-proportioned curves, someone who took care of herself and maybe played sport, rather than someone who intended to be particularly strong. She had brown eyes, with long blond hair tied back. She wore a multi-coloured summer top and short skirt, revealing her tanned figure to the full. Her clothes and jewellery looked expensive, designer attire rather than that of any high street store.

"Hi, I am Amelia Ellington. You must be Pete. I have something that you are interested in the purchase of."

Amelia held out her hand, and made a polite introduction, before entering the small cottage. She made herself at home in the small lounge as I offered her a drink, prior to sitting down in the cosy room opposite her. She spoke nicely, although not in a public school cultured accent, she did have a classy way with her. It was however a shock to meet her, she was young, only looking in her mid-twenties at most, although mature for her years. She was not the playboy banker whom I had expected. She totally blew away the stereotypical, thirty-something year old, cocky male, in the pin-striped suit from public school. She appeared to be well off, or portraying to be well off, but did not demonstrate any signs of having a habit to feed. She appeared calm, with a controlled, business like, considered, almost calculated manner. Although I had never met her, she did somehow appear familiar. I had either seen her somewhere on my trips to the island over the last few years, or she reminded me of someone whom I knew.

We exchanged pleasantries and had a lengthy chat about interests, our background, and life in general. It was in a friendly, inquisitive manner, almost in the way of someone who was trying to find out about someone at first meeting, trying to establish if this was a potential candidate for future friendship.

It was time to move on to the purpose of the visit. I wanted to get this whole trip over and done with, the frantic turmoil I was witnessing within was in danger of escaping from captivity at any moment. I had to remain strong, focussed on the task in hand. I realised that the friendly conversation, although with a total stranger, had a somewhat familiar edge. She was putting me at ease, almost inviting me to trust her, something that I knew that I needed to resist. It was a strange feeling, I almost wanted to confide my current situation in her. Maybe a friendly chat about a different subject was allowing me to release some of the pressure, reintroducing my mind to some form of normality. The world outside was continuing, its very existence had only ceased for me, something that I realised I had lost the concept of over the last few days.

"Sorry, may I just use the facilities please, before we move on to business?"

Amelia stood, smiled a caring, sympathetic smile and entered the bathroom. She turned on the tap before carefully climbing on to the top of the toilet cistern. Great care was exercised so as not to make any suspicious sound, as she removed the loft hatch above. Bonded to the timber at the side of the hatch, set within a generous amount of car body filler, was the Red Diamond. It was securely wrapped in plastic for protection, while being totally encapsulated. It took a little freeing from its position of concealment, secured in case any maintenance work was undertaken between the letting of the cottage to Emily and Sophie, until Pete's arrival. She broke the filler off the wrapping of the precious stone, placing it with the screwdriver which she had used as a lever, into her handbag. She then replaced the hatch while the toilet flushed.

Emily could not help but conclude from her conversation with Pete, that she approved of her sister's choice. Although he was not her type, she realised and understood the attraction and was pleased to have met him. She hoped that she had not over done the conversation and delayed the business for too long. She could not help herself, wanting to establish what the person she had heard so much about was truly like in person. She had tried hard not to let any of her prior knowledge of him escape during their discussion. She deeply wanted to come clean, to tell him that she was Emily Daniels, the sister of Sally Henderson and had only created the name Amelia Ellington moments prior to knocking on the door. She resisted the burning desire to tell him, or to attempt to plant a seed of thought in his mind about Sally, but knew she had to remain focused as she returned to the lounge and extracted the stone from her handbag.

"This is the beauty that I have sold to your colleague. I believe you are taking it for safe keeping tomorrow."

The deep intensity of the Red Diamond was for sure an item of beauty, but it was not very big. I could not believe that something so small could be so valuable. I was sure that Amelia would have been able to read the shocked expression on my face, surprised at the diminutive size of what I was told was a famous and valuable stone. I decided that as the deal was done, it was time to learn more, after all, she realised that I was only taking delivery of it, moving it to a place of safety.

"Wow, I love the depth of the colour. It is I have to say...rather smaller than I expected it to be."

"I have always been told that size is not everything. Besides, that must be over an inch according to my ex."

Amelia grinned and was clearly having a bit of a game, not something I expected from someone who had fallen on hard times and was now having to part with their precious collection to feed a habit. I knew that something did not stack up. Either Mark had been a little economical with the truth when asking me to move this diamond across a small island for a large fee, or Amelia was not in the position that I had been told she was in. The more I looked across at her, the more that I could see an element of familiarity in her. She also seemed a little too keen to turn this into a social visit, especially the way she appeared to be looking at me in an analytical manner.

"So what makes this little gem so famous then?"

Emily, was so wanting to come clean; not to tell the truth that the diamond was hot, but to reveal that she was Mark's daughter and Sally's full sister, despite the fact that she had her father's name, while her elder sister had that of her mother. She was seriously considering how to tell Pete, she liked him a lot in the short time that they had been talking, she felt that it was totally immoral that Sally had kept her life so divided. She decided as hard as it was that she must let Sally reveal her own identity. She so wanted Pete to be aware of the situation and help to ensure that Sally was safe. There had been no sighting or sound from her since she had left the penthouse. If only Pete had some degree of insight, then he could be prepared and help in some way. She also thought that he was looking at her with an element of disbelief being revealed within his eyes and his expressions. She was aware that he was clever and had been used to carrying out negotiations, so that he may have suspected something. Being asked to do a job by Mark in this way suggested that something may be of questionable legality, or at least have an added dimension.

"It is rare. Exceptionally rare, especially of this quality. About one in ten thousand diamonds have natural colour, it is thought that the chances of unearthing a true Red Diamond is; one in sixty million. Only around twenty in the world are officially classified as Red and not of red with another colour, most are less than half a carat. This one is a Round Brilliant Cut Fancy Red Diamond of 0.95 carat, thought to originate from the Alto Paranaiba region of Brazil. It was the first high quality Red Diamond to be sold at auction on the 28th April 1987 for $880,000 at Christies in New York. The jewel was thought to have been purchased by a Swiss Diamond Dealer representing the Sultan of Brunei, who is said to have one of the largest coloured diamond collections in the world."

"He probably has the largest car collection, too. I heard he owns around seven thousand, I would love to have a rummage through his garage."

"Well, rest assured, he does not own this; The Hancock Red Diamond."

"It has a name then?"

"Yes, named after its former American owner; Warren Hancock from Montana who died, which is why it went to auction. He is said to have purchased it in 1956 from a local jeweller for $13,500 – not a bad return was it? It is the intensity of the colour and richness that matter most, the carat and clarity come afterwards. This one is said to be the purest, most saturated in the world, it is quality rather than size that matters most."

"I always say that too."

The switches within my mind had changed the polarity of my brain, bringing forward images of the past, revealing why Amelia was familiar to me. I decided to take the plunge. I knew I had seen her around locally at home, she was no banker from Jersey, I recalled seeing her with Mark in a bar once or twice. In fact I was sure that Sally had spoken to her as if they were well acquainted.

"So if it is so famous and the Sultan of Brunei would hardly have sold it to raise some cash, how come you and Mark have it?"

"Mark who? It is mine, I am selling it due to the recession. I need the capital right now, but can start my collection off again when the economic climate is restored."

"Look, cut out the act shall we? You know Mark as well as I do, I do not know about a banker, you are trying to take me for a wanker."

I sat forwards and stared straight at Amelia. My stare fixed hard into her eyes without any flicker, or deviation from the epicentre of my focus. She smiled, looking almost relieved that the curtains had closed on her performance. She softened as she spoke, leaning forwards on the sofa, reaching across to shake hands for a new introduction, the second first meeting between the same two people in under an hour.

"You win, Emily Daniels pleased to meet you."

"Oh, Mark's daughter, it must be a big deal this one."

Amelia, sorry Emily, did not look particularly shocked, she remained cool and calmly admitted it was an act, realising that it was not necessary. We both found the funny side of it, with me taking the piss a little about the banker she had badly acted out.

We continued to chat. I was starting to like her as a person, and now that I had established that she was Mark's daughter we could chat in a more meaningful way. The truth also made the arrangements a little easier, I was able to establish directly from Emily where the little sparkling item was to go and what I was to expect. My concern was not mislaying something so precious, but something so small. I thought about the jewel who was far more precious, more beautiful and of a far higher quality, this was the one subject that I could not get her to discuss; Sally. Any mention of her was quickly dismissed no matter how much I tried, the subject was clearly closed. This fuelled my concern that was already out of control. I had a deep feeling in the depths of my soul, one that I could not explain, but indicated that something was wrong, very wrong and that Sally needed help. I was sure that there was a link to Mark, Emily and this little red gem.

Chapter 17

Delivery of Something

The sun faded into the sea as I walked from the beach with Emily. It was time for me to depart and conclude the transaction. It was decided that my mode of transport needed to be a little more suited to the selling of such a high value commodity. The little hired Ford Fiesta remained at the cottage with Emily. I took her hire car, a silver Mercedes SLK280; the classy convertible had been sitting in front of the little fisherman's cottage all afternoon.

With the jewel safely stowed away, I headed out of the gravel drive and onto the tarmac road to travel over to St Brelade. The purchaser's house was just outside the settlement itself, located on a country lane free from street lights. Under the cover of darkness I became paranoid about checking that there were no headlights in sight. I was sure that every other car on the road that was moving in the same direction, or waiting at the roadside, was there to follow me. Everyone was being considered a predator, not a person who simply frequently travelled the road to reach their own home. A car had been behind me for some time, but passed when I pulled in just after the drive to the house that I was looking for. I turned around after the tail lights had turned the corner, then proceeded down the drive, quickly being greeted with electronic security gates with voice entry. I made my presence known, the gates parting to allow my passage, I hoped that it was to be a safe one. A burning desire for the transaction to be over as quickly as possible was at the forefront of my mind, I had no idea what I was about to face. The drive curved round to the house lined with dense bushes on either side, the length illuminated by LED lighting.

I arrived at the front of the grand house, a large palatial villa-styled property with Corinthian columns, large arched windows and pastel coloured render being illuminated in the dark. I took a deep breath and walked to the double timber doors. As I approached, one door opened, I was greeted by a young Indian gentleman in a dark suit and turban. He looked me up and down without smiling or saying a word, then beckoned me in. I attempted to make small talk to break the ice, but there was still no response or acknowledgment as he led me into a room off the hallway. I sat where I was pointed to go and looked around the room. The hallway had been the full height of the property, painted gold with marble stairs and floor. Ornate antique furniture was dotted around giving a grand, continental feel. The room I was in was however something different again, the walls were painted a bright red with Indian finery spread around the large space. A table was set with gold rimmed glasses, but somehow not looking lived in.

The door opened and the purchaser himself walked in. A tall, smart man in his late fifties, dressed in traditional attire, wearing a Sikh ceremonial Kirpan. He smiled across to give a friendly greeting, although I could not help fix my eyes on the gold dagger, decorated with large jewels. I just hoped that this was for pure ceremonial purposes and it was not something that was intended to enter my body, following the Red Diamond being safely transferred to his possession. He did not look aggressive towards me and I convinced myself that he was not going to cause me any harm. I did not feel that a polished gold Kirpan with jewels set in it, and his traditional white attire, offered itself readily to the spilling of my blood.

Mr Singh greeted me politely in a cultured accent, with a slight Indian tone to his voice. He shook hands and sat down on the embroidered chair opposite the sofa that I had been positioned on. The man who greeted me closed the door then stood in front of them. I was unsure if he was being a good butler, remaining present, waiting to be able to serve his master, or if it was to intimidate and block my exit. I decided to try to establish a rapport with Mr Singh, but he headed straight into discussing the business.

"Your colleague visited me last week with the stone. A pleasant young lady I must say, mature beyond her years. I have the cash, now do you have something for me?"

He reached to the floor, opening a laptop bag and placing it on the coffee table. I looked at the contents that had been revealed, unsure how much cash was there, some were twenty pound notes, but the majority were clearly the rarer fifty. This was clearly some deal, although I was not aware of the figure, it was hundreds of thousands of pounds that was due to be entrusted to me.

I placed the Hancock Red diamond onto the coffee table that lay between us. I wondered if the old timber top of the table with its fine, intricate inlay had ever had something so valuable sitting upon it. The deep, ruby-red colouring of the stone glistened in the strong light from the Chrystal chandelier above us. Mr Singh smiled, beamed, his face lit up as he handled what was to be a cherished item. It was clearly to him a moment of joy, he was the proud new owner of the Hancock Red.

"Now we have concluded the deal, would you like a drink?"

I was wanting to get out of the room, out of the house and a little intimidated by the man staring at me from the door, but thought that it would be rude to refuse. The two men spoke to each other in their first language and for the first time he moved away from the door, although only for a few seconds, the time needed to relocate a silver tray containing labelled crystal decanters and glasses onto the table.

I sat back, drink in hand as Mr Singh rocked back in his chair and smiled. Not this time a friendly smile, it was one that was suggesting that he knew something and I had a distinct feeling that the knowledge was about to be shared.

"Your pretty colleague has misled me. She is selling me something that is not what she says it is. I realise however that she genuinely believes that it is what she has told me. I know better, I know what it is that I have. What do you say? Do you think therefore that it is I that is the one doing the misleading?"

"The Hancock Red? The most famous, of less than twenty certified, natural red diamonds in the world; do you mean?"

I was trying to sound informed and to look calm externally, but felt the blood draining from my face. Was this a trap? Was I indeed the courier of a stone that was not actually what I had been led to believe it was?

"The most famous, purest, deepest red diamond – yes indeed. The Hancock Red, however, no that is where you are wrong. I have seen it. I know its owner; the Sultan of Brunei. He purchased that gem a good few years ago now, still owns it in his collection, too."

I made no comment, I was too busy wondering what was coming next. I knew for sure that there would be no escape from this room, or from this situation.

"This, my friend is something else. Let me educate you with a little history shall I? The earliest known red diamond was a little larger than the Hancock, about 1 carat, it has the deepest colour of all and was discovered in the late eighteenth century. In the early nineteenth century it was sold, purchased by a diamond dealer in Parris by the name of Edwin Streeter. It then disappeared and was not seen again. A century later, a deep red diamond turned up that was 0.95 carat; most people assumed due to the rarity, that it was the same stone. The probability was that it was the same stone, but there was no proof. No proof at all, not due to the passage of time, but because it was not the same stone at all. This, young man, is the very stone that has been lost since the early nineteenth century; The Halphen Red."

I wondered what this all meant for me, my future and the deal.

"My friend, relax, you are looking most uptight. I have been looking, searching for this jewel for many years. I knew it existed and believed that it was in England, but had no way of locating it, or proving its existence for sure. Once the text books decide that two stones are in fact one, there is little interest in the first stone. This is the Halphen Red, the jewel that I have searched for over the years and not given up upon. Now you and your friend have found it. Where from I do not wish to know. You have delivered it to me. No matter where you stole this from does not matter, people will not look for the Halphen Red as it is believed to be the Hancock Red, which rest assured is safe and secure. I could not be happier. If ever I found a better one I could sell it at full value on the open market, saying it had been in my family since Edwin Streeter sold it to my ancestors. Lost for years, uncovered at last. Now I can compare notes with the Sultan of Brunei, but I think that I have the better of the two."

I sighed inwardly, relieved that it appeared that I was in the clear. I liked Mr Singh and his knowledge, I was pleased with the outcome as I left the end of his drive. I had the money for Emily, he had a more valuable little stone that was not really hot, as it was believed by many to be something else, and I was free. There was one massive crater, part of my heart was still missing, and news on the one thing that I wanted to be alright was still silent. My concern grew once more now that the pressure of my task was dissolved. I hoped that this would be a key to Sally coming home again.

I sat in the Mercedes near the top of a small hill that overlooked the sea. The monotone, muted colours turned into more recognisable shades, gradually the definition of the scene increased with the dawn light. I was there to think, to absorb thoughts from somewhere. A car passed by, screeched to a halt and started to reverse into a gateway near where I was parked. I started the engine, ready to drive in case this was someone who was to approach me. A familiar, muscle-toned young figure was heading in my direction yielding a knife. It was a guy whom I had seen around who worked for Mark; I was not sure, but thought that his name was Delroy. I was unsure if I was safe. Was he after me? Surely he was on the same side in all of this? Was he here to assist? Had Mark taken exception to something? I quickly swung the car around, he saw my face as I turned. He looked surprised, shocked, taken back and made no further approach. I pulled the car in, blocking his hired BMW X5 in the gateway, got out of the car, locking it as I headed towards him. He turned, ran, fleeing up the grassy bank that was overlooking the sea. I could not comprehend his action, why he was running from me and his reasoning for looking shocked.

I followed him ascending the bank, realising that he was probably expecting the car to contain Emily. I chased after him, calling him, wanting to know what was happening. He was tall, young, fit and strong, my Olympic attempt at a gold medal was fading from my grasp. The distance was increasing, all I could do was to keep going, believing that this was something to do with Sally. The chase felt like a dream. Have you ever walked up a hill in a scenic area, only to continue to climb the next grassy mound, eager to reach the summit that never arrives, you pass over the crest of the next hill, but another lies ahead? Or have you turned the bend of a cliff top path to see what treat lies in store ahead? The excitement of the surprise which awaits lies before you, but you are only to be greeted by another bend that needs to be turned, travelling further before reaching the greatest vantage point of the sea. In fact although running forwards with all of the determination that I could muster, it was like being on an outdoor, scenic treadmill, with the scenery moving backwards, not getting any closer. As hard as I tried, I had no chance of catching him and was simply out of breath. I turned, heading back to the car, confused at seeing him here, yet alone with a

knife. I realised that my presence in Jersey that Mark had been so insistent upon, may well ultimately be to help Sally.
I returned to the cottage. This was something that I needed to share with Emily, and quickly. I believed that Delroy was after her and had no interest in me, in fact, he was clearly not wanting any contact with me.

***

Sally looked across the caravan, desperately attempting to seek inspiration. Not long after her arrival, Armstrong had sent Delroy out for a reason that was unknown to her. It was something that she was somewhat pleased about, not just that he had left, but an opportunity to talk with the familiar DS.
"What do you want with me? I want to know what this is about. Look, we have known each other for years; you have worked well for my father, what is all of this? Why are you here with Delroy? He is not your type to deal with, you are better than him. He is just muscle and ego joined together, although maybe not in that order. You owe me an explanation at least, after all of these years."
Armstrong turned in the dim light to face Sally, she realised that as Delroy had left the boathouse, she had half a chance of sorting something out with Armstrong, rationalising the situation, hoping to do some sort of deal with him. This was something that she had successfully done from many a police cell when the tape recorder was switched off. The caravan was fairly old, well worn, but still in a condition that some people may be happy to spend a summer vacation within, while on the island of Jersey. Although maybe not the case when parked in a dark, damp, old boathouse. She realised that Delroy was a loose cannon, one who could not control his ego, or temper. She realised that she would be unpopular, being to blame for ensuring that his enemy; Lee Field was not residing behind bars like a caged animal for the next few years. She also realised that if he wanted to get back at Emily, she was a suitable candidate. The danger she was in with Delroy was all too apparent. She was alone, leaving no

message had meant that she could try to find Pete, but also that she herself would be hard to find, especially in a caravan within a boathouse. The danger was increasing minute by minute, the catalyst to her reacting with the world again, if ever, was Armstrong.

Armstrong still remained silent, although looked at Sally for a moment, before lowering his gaze.

"Detective Sergeant, you are doing nothing wrong here with me. All you are doing is keeping me safe, acting under cover, just like you have in situations over the years. You have found that Delroy is a head case, intercepted him, gained his trust and are going along with his plot to keep me safe before handing him in to the police. I know that, you know that. He is not here, we can resolve this and ensure that he is arrested. That is the truth, DS. That is the truth and you will be recognised, although coming out here on your own is more than a little maverick. I am sure the recognition will enhance your pension as you begin your retirement."

"Too late for all that, Sal. I am not interested in you, you know that. Delroy is, he will hurt you to get back at you for getting Lee off and to have a dig at your little sister."

"Dclroy docs not carc about Emily, all hc cares about is his image, the power, to be fucking the daughter of Mark. He will realise it is over between them and will soon realise that my father is not someone to upset, or to mess around with his little girl. He will realise, either that, or make his mark in history as a statistic. Come on, DS, let us find the station shall wc?"

"Your bastard father was pensioning me off, too. Not just the force, of course as soon as I retire I am off, superseded, an obsolete item of no use, or value to him. He pays people, he uses them, what good to him is a has-been copper? That is why I am here. Delroy is working for me, assisting me to get the golden handshake of the magnitude that I deserve from him. The money from that Red Diamond that Lee Field and his accomplice Sophie stole is what I want. I assume that your father's firm quoted for CCTV, an alarm or something for the property it was taken from."

"DS, my client Mr Field was cleared of all charges. He did not take any Red Diamond, or have the words of the Judge slipped your mind? You therefore are after money that does not exist, from a deal that does not exist, from someone who was not involved in any robbery and has no knowledge of any coloured diamond, yet alone a red one. Then as well as all of this fabrication that you have dreamt up, have you forgotten something; my father?"

Sally could see in his eyes that Armstrong was ashamed of what he was doing, but he had clear intentions. Intentions that she now realised were to be difficult to fluctuate. He was a desperate man. His gambling had been destroying his income at an alarming rate, now he was to retire from the force and from her father, he realised he could not afford his addiction. It was one that had grabbed him firmly, clenching him, coiling itself around him and squeezing. The python of betting had taken hold, its grasp was not to be relaxed. She could see that he was indeed the person behind all of this, although she believed that he would not directly hurt her, this was his plan. He was the instigator and that Delroy was just along for the ride and revenge, being used by Armstrong.

Hired muscle was all Delroy was good for, he did not have the sense for anything else. It was what her father had used him for and now what Armstrong was employing him for as well. She realised that Delroy would become a statistic, that his body would one day soon become an empty shell of muscle, parting company with his soul. She realised that she was, however, in great danger, as Armstrong had no intention of turning the tables on Delroy, someone who had it in for her, a desire to hurt, torture and maybe kill her without even realising the consequences of his actions. She knew that the consequences would find him quicker than he would realise, but that would not preserve her safety. As long as he was out she was safe, it did nothing but buy her thinking time and time for her to be found. Located within a caravan, contained within a boathouse, on an island that people did not know she was on; a simple task, it was not.

Sally stood, stepping to the door of the caravan, looking into the dark structure that it was concealed within, hoping desperately to find an easy exit. As far as she could see she had three options that she could follow; wait to be attacked, killed, or worse by Delroy; try to get through the large securely locked door of the boathouse; or climb the ladder to the floor above in an attempt to escape through the window to either the roof, or the ground below. At least the final option had one appeal, although it may result in injury, climbing through a window would summon attention from the tourists outside in the harbour, falling to the ground, screaming for help, or attempting to scramble to the roof would not be unnoticed. Even in a society of people consumed within their own lives and self-interest, such actions should, theoretically, highlight to someone that she had a problem. If she was noticed she had a chance of escape and sharing the knowledge that she was being held captive.

She felt safe with Armstrong not just through her involvement with him over the years, but because he was rational, he wanted only one thing; the cash. He realised that the key to the cash was her safety, without her, the cash had no chance of travelling in his direction. Delroy was not rational, but hot-headed, his priority would not be whatever small share Armstrong was paying him, but revenge, to inflict pain and suffering on her for freeing Lee. That very action would in turn, inflict mental pain on her sister when she realised what Sally had been put through by her ex-lover. She had to plan her actions quickly and before Delroy returned, Armstrong she could take by surprise, but she would not be able to overpower the strength, athleticism and hatred of Delroy.

Chapter 18

Travelling Fast

I was more puzzled than ever as I returned to the old fisherman's cottage. The surprise that had been etched on Delroy's face as he approached me in the car had become inscribed within my brain. As I walked towards the door, I noticed that it was ajar. Leaving the briefcase in the car, I cautiously pushed it open. I crept in, listening for any sound as I looked around the cottage. Nothing illustrated any forced entry or disturbance, everything was exactly as it was when I left, apart from one thing; no sign of Emily. I knew that Delroy would not have got there before me, even if he had another car waiting further along the coastline. I walked to the door, looking towards the beach I spotted the figure of Emily, she was walking towards me while talking on her mobile phone, her body language indicating that she was stressed. Spotting me, she ended the call and walked purposely forwards.

As she neared I could detect that her face had altered from before. The cool, calm exterior and friendly chatting had disappeared, replaced with a bluntness and hastened focus. I recited what had happened; she did not appear at all shocked with the news about Delroy and clearly did not have any interest in the name of the Red diamond.

"Never mind the bloody stone, hide the money in the loft, give me the car keys and stay here."

I was taken aback by her abruptness as I was given my orders. I knew something was wrong, seriously wrong and started to panic.

"Emily, is it Sally? What can I do? Tell me, fucking tell me!"

"Shut the fuck up. Stay here, have you got that? Stay here! Stay with the money, no wandering off. The best you can do is leave this to the professionals. If I need you I will call."

Her brown eyes hardening as they drilled into me, the temper being evident. She drove off in haste. I struggled to excuse her abruptness and the silence I was being subjected to on the one subject that I wanted to talk about. I was sure that it was the situation that she was annoyed with and not me personally. I had naively thought that the sale of the stone had gone well, that I had performed my function and that meant that everything would be alright. I was wrong, so wrong, in fact it seemed to be the inverse. The sale of the little jewel seemed to have trigged something, something of serious consequences.

My frustration grew inside of me as I concealed the cash, making sure I was on the lookout for anyone who approached the cottage. I walked through the garden and onto the tiered terrace that overlooked the beach with its old steps leading down to the sand. I sat facing side wards, a good vantage point. I could see the door of the cottage and the drive for anyone approaching, but at the same time had the full view of the beach. It was a pleasant place to sit and contemplate. When the tide rose invading the sand, stone and shells, smothering the rocks, submerging all but their tip, I would be able to wonder down to the revised shoreline, while the cottage would remain in view. There was nothing practical I could do. I knew that news would percolate into my brain at some stage. Either Emily, or someone would return with news, or Sally would find her way to me. At least I was at a cottage that we loved, in a position that we loved, I had to hold that thought, abusing it, exploiting it, to enable me to maintain my sanity and keep control of my emotions.

***

Armstrong decided to make a telephone call, it was something that Sally had been waiting for, until she witnessed the conversation that was.

"Emily Daniels. DS Armstrong here. We have your beloved sister. She is safe for now, but concealed. When you get the money from that little stone that your darling Sophie stole, you give it to me. All of it, let's think of it as my pension. That is all I want from you and your father. Not much to ask after all I have done over the years. A bargain. Now what do you say? Oh, just one other thing; Delroy. He will take care of Sally while you deliver the money and then I tell you where she is. No tricks though. No muscle, the sooner the better. Delroy does not care for your sister much, if you do not do exactly as I say, I will have nothing, and I accept that. But you will have no sister; Mark will have only one daughter. As well as being family, she is a bit handy when it comes to court and arrests is she not? Delroy will be happy, though, there is nothing that he would like to do more than have the satisfaction of having fucked both of Mark Daniels daughters, then halved the number of offspring he has. It is your choice. What do you say?"

Armstrong was silent, listening to Emily on the mobile while turning to look across at Sally, not taking his eyes off of her. Watching her expression, as she tried to conceal the fear of Delroy. She realised that Emily would try something, or her father would by now be on his way to the island.

"Fine, as soon as Delroy returns I will text you with the location. He will keep Sally safe, until I tell him otherwise that is."

The call ended, Sally realised that it was only a matter of time before something was going to happen. If she left now, while Armstrong was there she had no way of being able to warn her sister as she did not know where she was. If she waited, she realised her fate. She suspected that Delroy would carry out his intentions whether Armstrong contacted him to say the plan had failed or not. Sally turned and tripped in the dimly lit caravan, slipping towards the door. Crying out in pain as she tried to move on the floor, pulling herself up on one leg as she leant against the closed door. She held her leg, almost crying in pain.

"Sally what have you done?"

Armstrong moved towards her, revealing a degree of concern.

"I have hurt my ankle, please wet that cloth over there in cold water, to help ease the swelling?"

Armstrong obliged, turned to wet the cloth. As he did so, Sally opened the caravan door and fled, climbing the old ladder style steps on to the floor above. The upper floor was empty, the floor boards creaking even under Sally's light weight.

"You bitch, do not fucking trick me."

She could hear Armstrong starting to head up the steps. She moved to the small window on the gable of the boathouse as rapidly as she could. Forcing the dust layered opening casement she leant out, looking around, her eyes scanning, trying to take in the situation in all directions, frantically attempting to relay the image to her brain. She realised that she was under extreme pressure, having only had a couple of seconds to make a decision on which way to head; up, or down. She looked up to the roof, it was a greater distance to the eaves from the window on the gable than she thought. It left one option, one that she was not feeling happy about, that was down. She hoped that she had selected the best option, as she climbed onto the windowsill. Armstrong was now at the top of the steps and starting to transverse the room. She heard the splitting, cracking of timber, realising that he had put a foot through the weak floor, and it was enough to buy her time for her exit. He pulled his foot back up and continued across the room, as she lowered herself as far as she could by her finger tips off the outside of the window. She looked down, hoping that the length of her body was enough to reduce the impact of her landing, took a breath and let go.

She fell the distance to the cobble stone harbour below, rolling onto her side as her feet started to absorb the first impact of the ground. Armstrong moved back to the steps, almost sliding to the floor of the boathouse and opened the door. Running out he almost collided with a family heading towards the sea. He moved around them, the redness of his face deepening as he struggled to get his breath. He now had to cope with how stupid he felt in falling for a simple trick, after all of his years in the force. He turned the corner to the elevation that Sally had fallen from, hoping that she would be lying on the floor, not badly injured, but hurt enough for her to be immobilised. He looked around, turned the corner, there was no sign of her, only locals and tourists at the busy harbour and shops.

"What the fuck do you think that you are doing?"

Armstrong turned at the familiar sound of Delroy's voice and explained. Delroy punched the wall, not being able to believe that she had escaped. He ran down the road, looking around in all directions, desperately trying to spot the woman whom he hated. There was no sign.

"Del, there is only one thing for it. We act fast. I will text Emily the location of the meeting now, head there now. That way they are none the wiser, we get the money before Emily realises that her sister is free."

"Go on then. I will find her, rest assured I will get that fucking bitch! She will live to regret this, just let her see."

Armstrong got in his car, made the text to Emily and set off to the meeting point that he had suggested at one of the more isolated parts of the island. Delroy had adrenalin pumping around his body. He was on a mission, a wild, uncivilised animal, focused on nothing but hunting down his prey, no matter what the cost.

Armstrong got out of the car at the agreed location, looking around making sure that there was no trap, checking that he was alone and they were not to be disturbed. He did consider that maybe Sally in a way had done him a favour, it had increased the velocity of the proceedings, giving less time for Emily to think, or make arrangements of any kind. He had given her nothing but travel time in the text message, accompanied by a warning of the consequences if Emily tried anything, or did not make the venue on time. In fact he realised that she would have to move quickly to stand a chance of reaching the meeting on time. There was no way that she could achieve it by keeping to the island's 40 miles per hour speed limit. He looked around on hearing a car approach quickly, then come to an abrupt halt at the side of his. It was a silver Mercedes SLK, with the familiar image of Emily at the wheel. He watched her from the back of the car, taking some small delight in seeing her get out of the car, her short skirt stretched against her figure. Emily walked towards him, a laptop bag in hand, looking pale, taking a gasp of breath as she approached him.

Emily stood in front of Armstrong, the worry evident on her young face. Armstrong stared straight into her eyes. His face still reddened by the unexpected exertion of 20 minutes earlier.

"Do you have it in full?"

He looked around, making sure that they were not being watched. Emily nodded, looking straight at him, not moving her gaze, hoping to identify any sign of movement and predict any action.

"It did not need to be like this you know, if only your Dad had treated me fairly. He knows that he, you, Sally, Pete, Lee, Sophie and half of his staff are only free due to me. If it was not for me, the lot of you would be inside. Even if any of you had been released, you would be having a hard time of it. Such a shame. I was only asking for my wages to continue until the end of my days, a happy retirement is all that I was asking. I may have even taken relief from you as payment in kind some weeks if you were a bit short of cash."

The couple stood in the elevated position, enjoying the isolation of the cliff top, high above the sea at Gronez, the racecourse stood empty behind them. The gentle sea breeze helped cool the day as the rays shone down from the deep blue sky, the rocky outcrops forming a silhouette in the background, the sea, deep physically and in colour reflected from the sky was hitting the rocks below.

"Where is Sally? She better not be hurt. If Delroy lays one finger on her you will pay also."

"She is fine she is in a boathouse. You pass the money over to me, I tell you where."

Emily nodded and slowly moved the laptop bag in front of her, holding it out horizontally as she reached to undo the zip fastening.

***

Sally was pedalling free on the teenagers' bicycle that she had stolen, finding it leaning on the rainwater downpipe on the corner of the boathouse. She headed along the sea front towards St Hellier, following the pedestrian route, rather than the road. A few people had become a little upset as she frantically peddled the bicycle that was too small back along the coast, aiming for the old fisherman's cottage. She realised she had caused one too many near misses along the route and had hardly gone unnoticed. She was out of breath, her right hip and side was acing from her fall from the window and was attempting not to cry. She had pushed her body as hard as she could, only the adrenalin was fuelling her determination. She abandoned the bicycle and hired a taxi from the edge of St

Hellier. She reached her chosen destination, throwing a bunch of notes at the driver, not waiting to establish the fare, but way overpaying. Fleeing down the path that lead between the expensive sea front houses from the road to the sand as quickly as she could, she reached the beach. She knew she was only a minute or two from the cottage and indeed at the same point that she had viewed Pete from, prior to Armstrong taking her into captivity. Sally hoped he would be there, prayed that he would be there, thinking that it is the place he would remain if he realised she was missing and somewhere on the island.

***

Delroy was more wound up than ever, he was struggling to control his rage, almost reaching his elastic limit. Not only had that bitch escaped from him, but Armstrong had let it happen. He ran to the coast, looking all around, all he could see was a young, rounded boy, aged around five or six years old crying. His face was red, as the tears rolled down his face. His mother was comforting him as his father stared along the coast, looking irritated.

Delroy though someone would have seen something and turned around to face the tourists along the sea front.

"Police! Where did she go?"

Delroy called out, hoping someone would be keen to be a good citizen and provide him with an answer to the random question.

The man with the upset child stepped forward.

"A young woman with dark hair do you mean? She shot down the sea front on a child's bike clean knocked Bradley's ice cream out of his hand when the idiot shot past..."

The reply faded into the distance as Delroy, adrenalin fuelled, called on his strength, stamina and fitness to run after her. He knew it would be Sally, he knew he had the physical and mental strength to get her, too. No matter what it took he realised he would get to her. As he ran along the coast, tourists were looking around, some were hiring jet skis, others just sitting looking at the sea. In the distance he could just make out a figure, one causing chaos, a woman on a small bicycle riding dangerously fast towards St Hellier, people scattering and shouting at her as she flashed past. His goal was in site, all he had to do was to push on. He knew he could do this in the gym when there was no real target to aim for, apart from something that he had selected himself. This time he had his physical target to reach, he was motivated to push his body to the limit to catch her. The subject was with every step getting closer as he approached the town.

Chapter 19

Element of Surprise

Emily stepped forwards towards the spiky rocks on the cliff top, then turned with her back to the sea. Gronez has a dramatic wildness that other parts of the island do not have; it is a hard, rather than soft landscape that surrounded them, quite appropriate for the situation that they were now both confronting. Armstrong stepped to follow, his gaze making focus with the lap top bag to view the content which he so desired. He knew he was in the position of power, for once having control over one of the Daniels. Not only did he have the power of holding Sally captive over Emily, but he was on safe, sound land. Emily had compromised her position by standing with the cliff tops and sea behind her. If he lurched forwards, she would have to either use her strength to push against him, or take a few steps backwards towards the cliff edge. He had the opportunity to take care of Emily if she tried to deceive him and there was no sign of anyone around to witness.

Emily's eyes stayed focussed on Armstrong as he approached almost close enough to identify the magazines that were laid out in the laptop bag, while she slowly, carefully, in a controlled way started to lift the lid.

A large rock-like figure, as hard and solid as the surroundings, stepped forward from behind a rock, moving silently to stand behind Armstrong. The figure raised one large hand connected to an arm as powerful as a man's leg, resting it gently onto the Detective Sergeant's shoulder. Armstrong jumped, the hairs standing up on the back of his neck, his face showing to Emily a flicker of terror. He turned, breaking his focus from the laptop bag, to find himself looking straight into the hard face of Mark Daniels. Mark stood staring straight into his face, seeing the terror that was being revealed in the windows of his eyes. Mark did not speak, he did not need to say a word, he realised that. He remained outwardly calm, holding back the words that he wanted to say. The girl's farther realised he had Armstrong and that he would know what he was thinking, speaking words would do nothing other than wind himself up further inside. Mark was experienced in this type of situation, apart from his oldest daughter being involved, it was all part of the day job to him. The silence was part of the power, part of the image that surrounded him. He stepped forwards, Armstrong stepping backwards as Emily moved to the side, watching the proceedings. The detective now had no power, no control, no badge or fellow officers to hide behind. He was exposed and in all his years in the force the toughest person he had ever come across was standing in front of him. He moved backwards, looking around, hoping to find a route of escape. There was none. Mark kept close in front of him, grinning at him, enjoying seeing the terror in his eyes and his frantic moves, panicking to find an escape.

Armstrong had two options, stay to be ripped apart by Mark, slowly being made to suffer, or bow out taking a couple more steps backwards over the cliff. He would then be arrested and judged upon his whole life's actions by his maker, before securing his destination for eternity. He started to mumble something, the fright in his eyes turning to tears, his body starting to shake. He realised what he had to do. He stepped back a further two steps, his feet losing contact with the crumbling cliff top as his rounded figure plummeted down, bouncing off of the jagged cliffs into the depths of the sea.

"Dad! Dad, what have you done?"

"Not a thing Emily, I just stood there, never touched him in anger. Never even uttered a single word. He made his own choice, I am kind like that."

"Sally, what about Sally? For fuck's sake Dad! He says she is in a boathouse, probably with Delroy somewhere, it is a bloody island surrounded with water and boathouses damn it!"

"St Aubin. On the harbour front. Young Josh spotted Delroy earlier. He has gone down there."

Despite the situation and her panic, Mark spoke in a calm, controlled, almost matter of fact way to Emily. His tone of voice was almost that of suggesting that she had asked a stupid question. She should have realised that he would know the location of the boathouse and that everything was in hand. Emily looked relieved, but angry at her father. He was one step ahead as usual and she was ecstatic at the news that Sally's location was known.

She still however had a concern regarding Delroy, from a female perspective she realised that every second counted and Sally was still in danger. They had spent a significant amount of time together over the last few months, she was aware of what he was capable of. He was hot headed, aggressive, determined, never thinking about the consequences of his behaviour. She herself had witnessed his forceful approach to women, which would have overpowered most, not having the strength, position, attitude and confidence that she possessed. Sally would have less physical strength against him, although she had a tough, hard edge, it was in a totally different, business like, mental way, rather than physical strength in a contact situation.

***

I wandered from the terrace down onto the beach and stood at the edge of the rocks. The tide was now in, reducing the size of the beach, concealing the majority of the sand that had earlier been glistening in the sunlight. I could still view the cottage from the revised vantage point, but this time had the power of the swelling tide at my side. The sound of the water made a deep glug sound as it lapped the rocks. I paused to consider if there was anything that I could do which would actually be constructive. Desperately trying to search through my brain to piece together the fragments of what I knew, I hoped a priceless antique would be created from the shattered elements, despite most of the components being missing.

The deserted beach was still, the tourists having gone back to their hotels, only the sound of the sea and chattering of the birds broke the silence. I felt someone touch my shoulders from behind me, slowly, gently, in a caressing way, then start to clench my shoulders more firmly. It felt familiar, it felt like Sally, smelt like her perfume and skin. I knew it would not be, that my brain and imagination was running wild again, my senses reacting to what my brain wished to feel, hear and see.

I moved my hand to my shoulder to touch the point where I was feeling the contact. My hands made contact with fingers, long thin fingers, as I took them within my grasp. I turned to face the image that I felt my imagination had created; Sally was looking upset, but smiling at me. Her deep, dark brown eyes sparkling, showing relief that whatever had happened was over. We turned to face each other, full of emotion, grabbing hold of each other as tightly as we could, not wanting to be separated for a moment longer. A grasp that grew firmer and more frantic by the second. Tears were rolling down her cheeks despite the smiles, welling from within the darkness of her eyes. We were together, wanting to be as close as we could get, never wanting to be separated. If the moment lasted for ever, it would not be long enough. Neither of us uttered a word, our actions spoke louder, emotions too transparent to require further complication. We realised what each other was feeling and thinking, the moment had everything without the need to be interrupted by words, allowing us to concentrate on nothing but being together.

I felt a sudden intense pain in my back as I was pushed to the ground, firmly landing onto the rocks. The force had taken my breath, I gasped. I looked up to see Delroy grabbing Sally and hitting her in the face. The sound resonated through my body as I struggled to my feet as Sally screamed. My head was bleeding, I grabbed a rock, swinging it to pound Delroy on the head. The impact jerked his head to the side, cutting into his flesh. He lurched towards me and lashed out, hitting and pushing me with his free hand, while continuing to restrain Sally with his other. The impact knocked me to the side, I was struggling to keep my balance and remain on my feet, my determination swelling like my head as I went in for another attempt.

I was desperately trying to muster all my strength to fight him, restrain him, and prevent him from hurting Sally any further. No matter how much I tried his strength overpowered me, the frustration grew as I did not seem able to prevent him from hurting her. My strength was quickly diminishing through my failed attempts.

Sally was hurt; her face was also bleeding, the red fluid running from just above her eye. He was hurting the love of my life and I felt helpless. It did not matter what I did, how much I tried, my effort did not yield the result I intended. I felt helpless, no matter what move I tried it was yet again shrugged off by the power and fitness of Delroy. Sal was being hurt. Hurt. She was in pain. She was scared. I just did not seem to be able to help. I was the one person in the world who was supposed to be protecting her, helping her, keeping her safe and secure, but all my attempts were resulting in complete and utter failure. The feelings of frustration turned into desperation, evolving into failure, not being able to come to terms with how useless I was, how I could not regain any form of control over the situation. I struggled on, hitting out at him, looking around for driftwood or a loose rock that I could raise. There was nothing to immediate hand. Nothing that would help, nothing to amplify my strength. I looked further away for anything that I could utilise to assist my situation.

I could not believe how frantic I was getting. How helpless I was remaining. The theory of effort attaining results, that you receive results based upon what you put into something was not yielding anything positive. All theories were being proved incorrect. I simply could not overpower him. My anger grew, not just at Delroy for hurting Sal, but at myself for succeeding in nothing apart from proving that I was useless while she got hurt.

"You fucking bitch. I said I would get you for what you have done. Getting Lee off. I warned you, bitch, I warned you! Then you escaped, you cannot resist can you? You cannot stop yourself from trying to make a fool out of me. You and that fucking tart sister of yours. Why do you do it? Why do you do it? Why do you fucking do it? What is your problem with me? Why do you want to make a fool out of me? Why? Why? Why bitch? Why?"

Delroy was clearly losing all perspective of reality and sanity. I found the strength from somewhere to lift a large rock, maybe through temper, maybe through adrenalin fuelled from the situation, fuelled from the hurt that I was witnessing Sally feeling. He repeatedly hit her, pushed her in both the face and chest. I turned with the rock, struggling to hold it, not believing that I was being able to raise it from the ground and swung it at his head. He was knocked sideward, losing his balance, as the blood trickled through his short, clipped hair. He turned to me, lashed out. He hit me to the ground once more. This time I was disorientated, trying to focus, as I saw the deep blue of the sky and the outline of the rock, with bright lights before my eyes. I struggled to sit up, finding it hard to focus on what I had to do.

Delroy reached down to his pocket, slowly and steadily extracting a knife from it. The sunlight glistening off of the blade. The action was careful, controlled and at a speed that indicated that it was a movement that was intended to be seen, intended to scare and induce a heightened level of fright to both of us. An action that the smile upon his face revealed as something that he was enjoying. Sally gasped, turning pale, letting out a groan as he showed her the blade. He was now enjoying the torment, enjoying inflicting the mental pain upon us. I struggled to get to my feet, pushing myself off the rocks, my feet slipping through the sand. I had one thing left, one action to try, that of waiting my time until he made a move to attack her with the knife, then throw myself in front of her. I did not care, I needed to pay the ultimate sacrifice to save her. It was a risk, if I left it too late it would be Sally who was pierced by the blade rather than me.

"See the blade, bitch. I fucked your sister, she enjoyed it. Now it is your turn, I'm not dirtying myself, I'm using this."

He lined the blade up between her legs, ready to make an incision, then fell backwards onto the rocks. I had been concentrating my efforts on the situation, not noticing anything, apart from Delroy and Sal. Someone had dived in, at speed, with strength, power and speed to overcome that of Delroy. He was strong, a gym junky, using his youthful strength to overpower him at the last moment, the crucial time. My vision started to come clearer, my eyes beginning to focus as I regained my balance. It was young Josh who worked for Mark, the grandson of Noel, the boy whom I took to the shops the day of the explosion all of those years ago. It was the day I met Sal, the day my life changed into what it has now become.

Delroy was lying on the sand, young Josh restraining him, Delroy not being able to move, no matter how violently he struggled. I tenderly got hold of Sal, cradling her on the sand, trying to calm and reassure her. She was now in floods of tears and shaking, her whole body trembling with the shock, her heart racing as she gasped short, rapid breaths.

I looked around, Mark and Emily were at the side of us, watching over Delroy. Sal was safe, we were safe, and it was over. Josh walked away, escorting Delroy away from the beach. Mark and Emily checked that we were alright, helping us to the old cottage, then left. They gave us time to be together without any interference. Time that we needed to recover from the last few days.

Chapter 20

Reflections

We sat together in the old cottage, the relief and reality of the last few days starting to intensify. We had hardly let go of each other since the beach, desiring some form of constant contact, reassurance, love. I could not comprehend that the day would unfold to answer the questions within my mind, even answers to questions that I had not realised were lurking within the depths of my brain were to be answered.

"Pete, there is something that I have to say. I have to come clean. We need to talk. I have some explaining to do. I had all the best intentions, but have misled you. Let us start again, tell you who I am. Who my family is. I understand if you have a problem with it. You have every right to."

I held Sal, not wanting to let go, not wanting the moment to end, but at the same time was scared of squeezing her too tight so that she felt pain from her bruising. I was also scared of what she was going to say, not that anything would have reduced the intensity of love that I was feeling. The moment was tender, caring, sensual, intimate but not in a sexual way.

***

Elsewhere on the island, Emily was struggling to control her father. He wanted to torture Del, to kill him, to make him pay for not hours but days, for the pain that had been inflicted on his family. Emily struggled to control and calm him, knowing that he would take action that was not controlled. Action that was not thought through and considered, action that was not planned, but being imposed on the spur of the moment. She knew that this was dangerous, realised that they were away from home, that they had been close to one death and involved in activity on the island that was not totally legitimate.

What they could carry out at home where they were known, where their image provided them protection was one thing, but in a different area was something else. There was nobody outside of the family to hear of any trouble and come forward without any contact, protecting them with a new waterproof alibi. Back home respected people would approach the police; those in authority, those holding high profile business, legal and governmental positions would assist. They had helped people through the whole class system, in all walks of life. In addition to those wanting to help the Daniels, there were those who knew that they should for their own wellbeing, that they were in a position that left them no option if they realised what was good for them in the future. The long established network was back at home, not here on Jersey.

Josh was with Delroy. They were work colleagues. This was something that Josh was playing on. He was using it as friendship to assist Del. To attempt to control his ego, temper and mind. Josh was bright, young, and manipulative; a skill he had developed from an early age, passively taught by Emily, Mark, Sally and his old grandfather Noel. He was loyal to the family. There was no question of that. Delroy though, did not have the intelligence to realise that, not being able to read that it was a game. He was not aware of the family connection, he just considered him as a young apprentice in Mark's business, not the person whom he truly was. Not the person who had decided his career direction the day of the explosion.

Josh had made Delroy see reason, made him see that he needed to leave the island, realise that he needed to play it cool for the sake of the future. He had convinced him that the way forward was to retreat, keep his dignity. Delroy agreed to fly back home to Nottinghamshire, get a few belongings and go down to London for a while, keeping a low profile until his time would come.

"Del, mate, revenge comes in time. It comes to those who wait. Tempers are high after what that bastard Armstrong did, what he got you involved in, the lies he told you. He, an officer of the law."

Delroy boarded the flight back to East Midlands Airport with Josh. They parted company at the airport.

"Keep in touch, Del. May see you soon. I would get away from here, pick your stuff up and concentrate on making it in London. Your time will come. You will get what you deserve. Believe me, you truly will in time."

Delroy interpreted the words that Josh had spoken in a positive way, not realising the true, intended meaning behind them.

Josh returned to the office to catch up on the happenings back home. He was pleased with himself, realised that he had followed the correct career path, pleased to give something back to help Sally and Pete who had shown him the direction from a child.

Del returned to his Mercedes Benz C Class coupe, threw his belongings into the boot and flung open the wide door in temper. He started the car, moving off quickly, not being able to believe what had happened. Heading from the airport he was pleased to escape; now all he had to do was to lie low for a while in London, waiting for things to cool. He was relieved that Josh had safely escorted him back home away from the Daniels, but annoyed at Armstrong. He felt that he should have known better and gone it alone to target that bitch, not joining in with the plans of an incompetent detective. Driving along the A453 he noticed the wanker's Racing Post sitting at the side of him in the car. It was a reminder of what had happened. A reminder of the life that he was putting behind him for a while.

He pulled into the lay-by, picked up the paper and pressed the cigar lighter into its socket to heat, he grabbed his knife, stabbing it forcefully into the rolled up paper and twisting it around. He reached for the lighter to burn it. Implementing the actions that he would have done to that bitch if Armstrong had not let her escape. He felt the chain around his neck tighten against the black leather upholstery. It was a feeling that confused him at first, alone in the safety of his own car. He raised his hand, thinking it must have got caught in the seatbelt, then glanced at the reflection in the rear view mirror. Hard, steely blue eyes were piercing into him, from the back seat of his own car, they were surrounded by a wrinkled, hard worn face, topped off with short, spiky hair. He absorbed this last image and gulped his last breath as he realised that Lee Field had got him for good.

"Good girl that Sally. No one at all messes, hurts or upsets her while I am breathing. Well, not and survives their action anyway. Fact."

Lee was as calculated and as brutal as ever. Waiting in the car for Delroy, then killing him was an action which generated delight. Sally meant a great deal to him, he was as tough as Mark, but a more brutal character, one who preferred to mostly work alone. Lee had no graces, what he thought, what you saw, was what you got. Things were clear to him, he was not strategic, seeing only black and white, implementing an action then moving on to the next.

***

I sat at home, normality had returned at last. Alice was running around the house playing her CDs, laughing hysterically while making 'hooo hooo hooo' sounds like a monkey. I now realised why I am in the position that I am.

Why I am paid what I receive. How I had gained the lifestyle that I have. In reflection it was obvious. What I was unsure of was how much of what I did was actually real, playing a part in a task for Mark and how much was an act? Like the image of the family, what was real and what was perception was something that I still struggled to comprehend, especially after the recent explanations. What I did realise though, was that I was under her umbrella, the umbrella of Alice; Mark's granddaughter and Sally; his daughter. They were protecting me. They provided the shield of the Daniel's family, the image that they had was projected over me. I had become one of them.

The telephone rang, I lifted the handset. It was the all too familiar voice of my future father-in-law.

"Now then, pal. How about a classic car run to the South of France? The Gorge du Vernon crosses the scenic Lac de Ste Croix, it is real driving country looking 700m down on the river. You will be twisting along the foothills of the Alps, top down in that MGB you have just purchased..."